CTHULHU,

PRIVATE

INVESTIGATOR

& OTHER STORIES

Also By Dennis Liggio

New Avalon Novels

I Kill Monsters (Nowak Brothers #1)
Jabberwock Jack (Nowak Brothers #2)
Support Your Local Monster Hunter (Nowak Brothers #3)
The Ghoul Pit (Nowak Brothers #4)
Manic Monday (Dane Monday #1)
Burning Monday (Dane Monday #2)
Murder Monday (Dane Monday #3)
The Case of the Dead Girl in my Apartment (New Avalon Case Files #1)
The Case of the Ghostly Runners and the Tall Man (New Avalon Case Files #2)

The Damned Lies Series

Damned Lies
Damned Lies Strike Back
Damned Lies of the Dead 3D

The Lost and the Damned
Paper Moon
Voices of Madness
Cowards And Killers
Cthulhu, Private Investigator

www.dennisliggio.com

Cthulhu, Private Investigator & Other Stories

By Dennis Liggio

www.dennisliggio.com

To Lovecraft and Hammett
And everyone who is okay with the idea of combining them together
Like chocolate and peanut butter

Table of Contents

Cthulhu, Private Investigator
1

It was the case I didn't want. I had even refused it. But when your partner ends up dead, his body floating at the docks, you're involved whether you want to be or not.

The case started with a woman.

When she walked in, I was sitting in my detective office in R'lyeh. My partner Dagon sat at the desk across from me. We had been doing the detective thing for a couple of strange aeons now. It was good for a few laughs while we waited for R'lyeh to rise again. A good dream always takes the edge off a long sleep.

We first heard her heels as they clicked down the hall. Next was her silhouette as she knocked on our door, the one labeled with *Cthulhu & Dagon, Private Detectives* in gold lettering. Then she came in, all hips and legs, swaying with the clack of her stiletto-heeled feet. She was trying the good girl act, but it was at odds with her clothes. She was dressed up like she just left the corner where she was selling sex to wayward church goers.

I knew Dagon went gaga for what she was putting out, but I had seen it all before. Behind the lipstick, the cleavage, and the mascara around half a dozen eyes, it was still her. I had dealt with Shub-Niggurath before and knew not to trust her, no matter her come-ons, the trill of her tongues, or the ever present sex bomb act. She had no loyalty to anyone except herself. She was the black widow type: use them up and take what she needs, the knife in their back optional. She had been around the block for more aeons than I could count. You don't get the nickname *The Goat with a Thousand Young* without getting around.

"I need your help! A book has been stolen from my cultists!"

She tried to make it a sob story, but her story stank like last week's dinner. There were too many holes, too many inconsistencies. It was a story for suckers. It was the hook and she was trying to reel us in. I could tell she wasn't trying to sell it with truth, but instead with a few pairs of long legs in nylons that were poured into red stilettos.

The way she told it, someone had stolen the Pnakotic Manuscripts from her cultists and she needed us to help get it back. As she batted her multitude of eyelashes, she explained that without that book, she couldn't be summoned to Earth and she was effectively blocked from the world ending apocalypse we all yearned for. This was a lie, since I could think of three other books off the top of my head which could summon her to Earth, and that's not even counting the Necronomicon itself. Then again, I think we had all learned to not rely on the hot potato that is the Necronomicon. You could maneuver your cultists into obtaining it and a week later it would be gone, either stumbled upon by a damned Miskatonic professor or willed to some ignorant relative upon the cultist's death. That thing has a mind of its own.

So I listened to her story, mentally knocking down every detail and argument she had, but not interrupting. I wanted her to go on with her whole spiel, pitching for the suckers she thought we were. She was too smart to have missed these details - when you're a vast immortal intelligence from endless spaces beyond the ken of mortal man you tend to not just get facts wrong. She was baiting a pretty big hook, I just couldn't figure out why she wanted to catch us.

When she was done, I said no. I was curious what she really wanted, but this was Shub-Niggurath. I wouldn't have trusted her to not have an ulterior motive if she asked whether I wanted milk or sugar in my coffee. No matter how this played out, we'd be the losers. Were we to be fall guys or just pawns? Or was this all just a trap? Either way, the answer was no. You don't investigate a trap by getting inside it. No thank you. As far as I was concerned, this was a job for one of her thousand young.

"No deal," I said. "You know better than to come here."

Dagon looked like he wanted to say something but he didn't.

"I assure you, I can pay," she said. "I can double your normal rate."

"Dollars are useless to dead man," I said. "Come back if you're willing to tell us the truth."

"I assure you, everything I have told you is correct," she said.

"Tell me another one, sister," I said.

So she left, a frown of disdain stretched across most of her mouths. She left her card in case we changed our mind. I immediately tossed the card in the trash. I heard the clack of her many heels as they receded down the corridor and out of the building. I turned over to Dagon and we laughed about it, though I laughed more than he. He had never dealt with Shub-Niggurath before, which was his downfall. I started drinking and listening to the radio, my legs up on the desk. Dagon read the racing sheets but seemed nervous. I took a short trip to the liquor store, and when I returned I saw Dagon nervously hanging up the phone. Neither of us said anything about it and a short while later he made some excuse to leave. I was alone in the office, the sun going down, but my liquor cabinet restocked.

Left alone, I overindulged myself, throwing shot after shot down my throat while holding back my quivering mouth appendages. I didn't head home but instead passed out in the office. I slept and dreamed in my usual fashion, dancing in the dreams of my cultists and enemies, manipulating the seas and storms for the day R'lyeh rose.

I awoke to the phone on my desk ringing. Through the haze of alcohol and century long dreams I reached out a clawed and scaly hand to pick up the receiver. My head was throbbing and my vision was blurry.

It was the police. They wanted me down at the docks or they were going to bring me in on charges.

Dagon was dead.

2

The docks were swarming with the police, like flies on crap. I mused that one good wave could wash all the filth away. Two detectives headed up the investigation. They were Elder Gods slouched in trench coats, waiving golden elder signs like badges to keep us Old Ones in line. Hypocrites. They were all crooked and they knew we knew it. They just glowed a little brighter than us, levitated a little higher than us, and for some inexplicable reason sometimes helped humanity.

The detectives were accompanied by five Hounds dressed as blue uniformed police officers. Hounds of Tindalos are practically unstoppable when normally set on their prey, but at the beck and call of the Elder Gods they're even worse. If the police wanted you, the Hounds would make it nearly impossible to evade capture. I hate cops. They weren't particularly fond of me either.

As evidence of this fact, they started accusing me as soon as I got there.

"Why'd you do it, Cthulhu?" said the shorter of the two detectives.

"I didn't do it," I said.

"Where were you last night?"

"Passed out in my office. I can't leave R'lyeh, as you know."

"Anyone see you there?" he asked.

"Only a bottle of whiskey," I replied. "And why would I kill my own partner?"

"Who knows with you Old Ones? You're all sick in the head. Who knows why you do anything?"

The taller Elder God gave the shorter one a look and the latter dropped that line of questioning. I was glad for that. Unfortunately, when a flat footed Elder God wants to harass you, there's not a lot you can do but sit there and take it. Now if they were willing to put down their elder signs and not use the Hounds...

Instead I looked down into the water. If I had any doubt that it was really Dagon, seeing his bloated corpse floating in the water, his many appendages hanging loosely, convinced me. He had been shot three times. Three times *in the back*. There are few deaths more undignified than being found floating dead in the water without having even had the courtesy of seeing who killed you.

"That is not dead which can eternal lie, and in strange aeons even death may die," I muttered as I stared at the corpse.

"Well, he's still dead right now, so he's kind of our problem, ain't it?" said the shorter detective, who must have overheard me. "One of you clowns bump each other off, and we got to cart our asses down here and figure it out. Next time you guys decide to muck things up, how bout you kill everyone and make our jobs easier?"

The taller Elder God put his hand on the shorter one's shoulder and then shook his head. The little detective relaxed and went back to questioning the dock working cultists. They didn't see anything. They never see anything - not even the cultists who weren't ritually blinded.

"You've got three days," said the taller Elder God. "Get us his killer within three days, or we'll pin this on you, Cthulhu."

"Aren't you going to investigate?" I asked.

The Elder God laughed. "That's a good one. You're a funny guy. Three days." He hovered off toward his partner. The uniformed Hounds were still sniffing around.

This left me staring at the corpse. I'd like to say that I went back to the office and just got drunk on cheap whiskey and distilled souls. I'd like to say that I had no idea what got Dagon killed. But I was positive it was the Shub-Niggurath case. Dagon got roped in by a pretty face and a story full of holes, and it had got him killed.

I had no evidence though. But since I was at the docks, I reached out to all the Deep Ones and asked them to check their network to see if anyone had seen Dagon or Shub-Niggurath in the last day. They would get back to me if they had something.

3

Back at the office, I found Shub-Niggurath's card on Dagon's desk. That confirmed my intuition. He had dug it out of the trash and called her. That poor fool had gotten involved with the wrong woman and it killed him. I didn't want to be the one to break his death to his wife.

I dialed the number on Shub-Niggurath's card. It rang a few times and then was picked up by a surly old man who spoke broken English. I held back frying his brain with madness long enough to learn that it was actually the number of a laundry in downtown Kadath, but there had been a strange woman there yesterday, waiting for a call. He said she paid money to reserve the phone for that time. I hung up, the old man finally gibbering insanely. I frowned my face tentacles. A temporary phone number. She had always expected us to call. Since it was not a permanent way to reach her, it was also clear Shub-Niggurath had always expected to burn us.

I took the stairs down to the street. I knew I needed to pound the pavement for a lead, but I had no clues that didn't bring me to the corner bar and the bottom of a glass that was two parts whiskey and one part souls. The bartenders at the Mouth of the Reef Inn knew me well and were always willing to extend a line of credit for me. It was at the bottom of said glass that a kid that sells newspapers found me. At first I tried to wave him off - there's not a piece of news that matters to a man with a dead partner, an empty glass of whiskey, and no leads. But he said it was about Dagon.

Looking the kid over I realized he was one of mine - the Innsmouth Look was smeared across his face like clown makeup. Not a Deep One himself, but their blood ran in his veins. His mother or grandmother had been a Marsh, I was sure of it.

His message was short and to the point. Dagon had been spotted going into Club KIY the night before. There were no other sightings of Dagon or Shub-Niggurath. The Deep Ones confirmed what I already knew - Dagon had not been home last night.

The plot thickened. I slipped the kid a fin and settled up my bar tab. As I headed over to Club KIY through a gate I opened, I wondered about the significance. KIY meant Johnny Hastur was involved. Nothing went on there without his involvement.

Johnny Hastur was a former Carcosa crooner, nightclub owner, mediocre actor, patron of the arts, and Old One of ill repute. He had ties to most smuggling operations through the worlds and was the primary cause any time an actor went insane. He was the owner and operator of Club KIY. Formerly called the King in Yellow after Hastur's damned play that none of us wanted to see, it was rebranded as Club KIY last year. Hastur wanted to try capturing the high society crowd. The interior was decorated in garish tones of yellow and artifacts of a vague Oriental suggestion. Despite carrying the title of the King in Yellow himself, Hastur was never seen in anything other than a white tuxedo and a white bonded smile.

I entered the club and swept past the bouncer. He knew better than to trifle with me. Oh, he could slow me down and cause me some grief, but in the long run he was better letting me pass and just telling his boss I was there. Inside, the rebranding didn't seem to be working as well as Hastur would like. In the late afternoon it was still frequented by drunks, insane artists babbling about their latest works, Hastur's own cultists, and a couple of Hounds of Tindalos off duty. Maybe it became more high society as the evening went on.

As I hit the bar for a drink, the house band, *Erich Zann and the Crawling Chaos*, took the stage. The stage was the one feature that dominated the club and which Hastur had kept through the rebranding and redecorating. Nowadays it played more big band music and waltzes to capture the upper crust crowd. His one concession to ego was that it still played at least one performance of the King in Yellow play per week, though from what I understood, those were at very non-peak hours.

I swiveled in my chair, holding my drink to get a better look at the clientele. I did see Bokrug at a table. Though technically an Old One, you wouldn't know it. Instead you'd just see a giant lizard stuffed into a cheap suit. Even with the suit he looked like a blockhead. He stared at me with unblinking reptile eyes over his drink. I didn't know who he was working for, but he was watching me intently enough that I made a mental note. I raised my glass to him, but he didn't return the gesture.

I also saw a couple of goons from Azathoth's bunch. I wasn't sure what they were doing here. It's not that they weren't allowed to have a drink wherever they wanted, but they had their own cult's places for that. And last I heard, Johnny Hastur had never been a friend to Azathoth's mob - they were far too blunt and violent for Hastur's refined tastes. Of course, we all knew that if we ever needed to bolster our own forces with cheap muscle, Azathoth was willing to hire his men out. He was pretty ambivalent to our struggles. Hastur had always loudly wondered if that neutrality was because he was more blind or more idiot, but I knew better than to second guess Azathoth's motives.

Speaking of the yellow devil, Hastur seemed to materialize next to me, his tux perfect, his smile gleaming.

"Hail, Cthulhu," he said. "So what brings the Lord of the Oceans to my humble bar?"

It might sound like he was polite and full of deference, but he was doing his best to insult me. Hastur and I have never quite seen eye to eye. Some might suggest we've been rivals for aeons, like brothers in an endless competition, but that's just dramaticizing the truth. We run in different circles, we have different cults, different followers. And he has never stopped hounding me to see his goddamn play. The only art I've been ever interested in is the curve of a woman's legs as she lays on the floor gibbering in madness at the sight of unfathomable space and the inevitable destruction of her world at my hands.

"Just having a drink," I said, raising my glass to clink against his, which seemed to materialize in his hand. If you're curious, he was having some sort of girl drink.

"And I wondered if you had come for the play," he said with a white smile.

"I'm never here for the damned play, Johnny."

"I thought your partner was here for it too," he said.

"Oh, did he sit in for a performance last night?"

"I thought he was going to, but then he left with a woman that wasn't his wife," said Hastur with a smile. "I wonder how that worked out."

"Poorly," I said. "He was found dead at the docks this morning."

Hastur's reaction was calm. There was no shock. Either he was the one who did it or he already knew about it from his own informants. Of course, there was also the possibility he didn't give a damn, but I think it was a big enough event that he'd at least be intrigued.

"You wouldn't know anything about that, would you, Johnny?"

He grinned again, trying to be genial. "Only what I hear from the word on the street."

"And what's the word?"

"That he's dead."

"Cut the crap, Johnny," I said. "He was here, he left and now he's dead. What do you know?"

"Oh, nothing of great interest," he said, swirling the straw in his drink. He was enjoying having me on the hook.

I simply glared at him until he responded. Hastur sighed dramatically, as if I was causing him great inconvenience. I considered grabbing his neck and slamming his head on the bar and then devouring whatever was inside his head but decided against it.

"I know that they left through the back alley," he said, pointing at a door in the corner. He took a drink through his straw. "And I know a nightgaunt followed them."

I raised an eye ridge at Hastur, but he simply stared down into his drink as he sipped it through the straw. Nightgaunts were always around, but they usually don't get involved in our affairs. They don't quite serve any of us, though we might get them to do some work from time to time. A nightgaunt was a wonderfully vague person to have followed them. If it was a servant or a cultist, it would have been much

Dennis Liggio

easier to determine their allegiance and know who was interested in following Dagon. That assumes it really was Dagon they were following and not Shub-Niggurath.

"That's all you know?" I said.

"All I saw," Hastur said noncommittally.

I was pretty sure he wasn't telling me something, but I didn't have anything to dig with. "I'll be back if I find you're lying."

"Come back anyway!" he said cheerfully. "Come see my play!"

I grumbled as I went out the back door of the club.

4

The back alley was what I expected. Trash and dumpsters. A kitchen staff member smoking a cigarette rushed inside when he saw me. I'm sure he didn't want to spend more time with me than necessary. That was fine with me, I wanted the privacy.

There was a wide open space right behind the club, then a long alley that then opened into a fairly busy street. Why hadn't any of my cultists or Deep Ones seen them leave? I should have heard something by now.

I had my answer when I stumbled over something buried in the trash bags. I saw the scaly foot first, then moved bags until I could see. It was a Deep One. Its cold scaly flesh was even colder than usual. It had been shot, that part was obvious. That explained why my network of informants had failed me. Someone was either keeping me in the dark or had found the Deep One watching and didn't want a witness.

I knew I could no longer trust my network of informants. Who knows how many others had been bumped off? If I could still get information from the network I'd have to take it with a grain of salt.

I walked out to the street and watched the kaleidoscope of cars in front of me, a countless array of stars that were never right. You could go anywhere from here. Catch a cab, a trolley, or just open a gate to your final destination. Dagon and Shub-Niggurath could have gone anywhere from here before ending up at the waterfront.

5

Heading back to my office, there was at least some good news. On the stoop I got nudged by that same newsboy informant. They had gotten a real address on Shub-Niggurath, a flophouse on the other side of town. I smiled at the news. As I entered my office, I was almost in something resembling a good mood until someone hit me on the back of my head.

My assailant had been standing behind the door in my office, so when I walked in, they struck. A hit to the back of the head was not enough to knock me out, but I stumbled forward against the desk. I heard the hammer pull back on a revolver, so I decided to take the next moments very carefully.

"Don't move," said my assailant. That I could do very easily, my head still smarting. Once he was sure I wasn't going to pull something funny, he said, "Okay, turn around and put your hands flat on your desk."

I turned so that I was leaning against my desk, my clawed hands palm down on it. He switched on the light, but I didn't need the light to confirm who it was - it was Yog-Sothoth.

Yog-Sothoth is often called the Lurker at the Threshold which might explain why he was hiding behind my door. He didn't have a nightclub like Johnny Hastur or a criminal empire like Azathoth, but what he lacked in entrenched power he made up in information. Yog-Sothoth was a twitchy worm of a lowlife, but if there was something worth knowing, he would know it. The question would be how much he was going to charge you, and of course whether he'd tell you or just lie. Since he was the Old One information broker, it was even more shocking when he didn't know something.

"Where is it, Cthulhu?" he almost shouted at me, the revolver rattling nervously in his hand.

"Where's what?" I said playfully. Truthfully, I had no idea what he was talking about. Was he talking about the Pnakotic Manuscripts? Shub-Niggurath gave me that line, but I doubted it was actually involved.

"Don't screw with me! Where is it? I couldn't find it!" he said. I looked around. My office was half ransacked. My footsteps must have interrupted his search.

I said nothing and stared at him calmly. After a few moments he relaxed, running an appendage over the glowing sphere that was his head, wiping off multidimensional sweat. "Look, I'm a reasonable god," he said. "What about if I buy it from you? Twenty grand for it. That's a fine price for it."

"Twenty grand?" I said, playing along, though I still had no idea what he was truly talking about. "That seems a little low for it."

"But it's of no used to you!" he said, but then seemed to choke down that line, as if he had said too much or he wasn't being truthful. "Twenty-five grand. You're not going to get a better price from anyone else."

"Oh, I don't know," I said. "Maybe I should ask them. See if they want to give me a counter offer."

"Don't screw with me!" he shouted, the revolver shaking in his hand, his glowing head orb pulsing with every word. "I'm walking out of here with it, whether you get paid or not."

He began pacing across the room rapidly, every so often kicking something or knocking an item off of Dagon's desk with his arm. The drawers had already been emptied on both desks, so there wasn't much else to overturn, but he was making sure every last object was tossed on the floor with extreme prejudice.

"You're not going to find it," I said. "I don't have it."

He stopped and stared at me with a petulant glare. Then he walked straight up to me, the revolver up in my face. "Unbutton your jacket."

"I appreciate the offer, but I'm just not into you."

The revolver in my face shook and spittle splashed across my face like a light rain. "Open your damn jacket so I can search your pockets!"

I mock sighed and started very slowly opening my blazer. As I began to pull the jacket open, I yanked my arms up, knocking his out of the way. I slammed my forehead down on his glowing head sphere. The gun clattered to the floor, thankfully not firing. Yog-Sothoth reeled backward. I finished him with a punch to the gut, his unconscious body falling to the floor. His glowing head sphere looked like it might have been cracked.

Picking up the gun, I eased down the hammer and checked the cylinder. Five bullets and an empty. It hadn't been fired recently. I put the gun in my pocket. I used Yog-Sothoth's unconsciousness to search his pockets for clues. Unsurprisingly, he didn't have twenty-five grand on him. He had a punched bus pass, some assorted change, some extra bullets, a pair of eyeglasses, and interestingly, a matchbook from Club KIY. I didn't find anything which might give me clues to what he was searching for and why I had it.

I pulled my chair around and sat down in it, pulling the gun from my pocket. I waited for him to regain consciousness. I poured myself a glass of whiskey with some cubes of frozen souls and waited.

Yog-Sothoth was groggy when he came to, but he tensed up real quick when he saw the gun pointed at him. I didn't make the mistake he had and kept myself a few feet away from him. When he tried to stand up I told him to stay on the floor until I said otherwise.

"You're going to answer some questions for me," I said.

"Gladly," he said, looking at the gun.

"What is it that you think I have?"

"You don't know?" he said with shock. Then to himself: "He doesn't know!"

"To be fair, I'm going to know in a few seconds because you're going to tell me," I said.

"The final legacy of Randolph Carter," he said. "They've finally found it."

"The Silver Key?" I suggested.

"Yes! Yes! The Silver Key!" he said with manic glee. I guess when you've lurked around a threshold for a few strange aeons, you get excited for gate-opening keys. Of course, that didn't mean he wasn't as nutty as a fruitcake otherwise.

"Why would you think I would have the Silver Key?" I said. Truthfully, unlike most Old Ones, I had no use for the Silver Key. I was simply waiting for R'lyeh to rise. That was my ticket to Earth.

"Because Dagon had it!"

"Dagon is dead," I said bitterly.

"Yes, yes, but before that he had it," said Yog-Sothoth.

"So it was taken off his corpse," I suggested.

"I have it under good authority that he did not possess it when he died," he said, not meeting my gaze.

"You killed him?"

"Oh, no, of course not," he said, a vague apology in his tone.

"Who did?" I said.

He said nothing.

"Who did?" I said more forcefully.

"I don't know," he said, probably lying. "My information is second hand. But I do know that everyone who could have done it is still looking for the Key."

"Everyone? Why are so many suddenly looking for it?"

"There was a deal last night," he said. "A man known as the Dreamer was selling the Key. I was authenticating the purchase of the Key for... an interested buyer. But Miss Shub-Niggurath showed up with Dagon and she wanted to make a counter offer. The true buyer suggested that it wasn't an auction, they fell to words and... well, get a bunch of Old Ones together and they all think they can have their way, right? I blame cultists. They do anything we ask, and nobody ever challenges us -"

"Get back to the deal," I said. "What happened?"

"It went bad, really bad. Naturally, I retired to someplace safer as soon as it started, but I can tell you from all the noises it got pretty violent. I don't know the exact details, but Dagon made off with the Key. Without Shub-Niggurath, mind you. Hours later he pops up dead and without the Key."

"And naturally you thought you could shake down me for it, since he was my partner?" I said.

"Naturally," he said without a hint of shame.

"Unfortunately, you're not in luck, since I don't have it."

"I know that...*now*," he said.

"So I'm going to keep this gun," I said, turning it in my hand, "and you're going to get the hell out of my office. If I see you again and you don't have new information for me, I'm going to fire first." I gestured to the door with the gun.

He scrambled to his feet, wiping dust off his suit. Then he awkwardly made for the door. When he had the door open, I called out to him.

"Yog-Sothoth," I said. He turned to look at me. "Who killed Dagon?"

He simply smiled nervously, saying nothing. Then he left.

6

Now I had even more of a reason to see Shub-Niggurath. I left my office about nine in the evening. I took a gate to the flop house my Deep Ones had located. It wasn't quite the high class hotel I would expect from her preferences, but if she was trying to hide out, she might pick a seedy joint like this.

I knocked on the door of 11B, at the end of a long hallway. This place had the look of a well-worn shoe - broken in and still warm from the calloused heel they just pulled out of it. Peeling walls, scratched up doors, dented and broken light fixtures - it had it all.

The door opened as far as the security chain would allow it. A multi-eyed and multi-mouthed Venus with a Veronica Lake haircut, Shub-Niggurath looked the femme fatale even in this dump. After her first look, I was sure she was going to shut the door and keep it locked. Her second look caught Yog-Sothoth's revolver pointing at her through the gap. She smiled weakly. The door closed slowly and the security chain was removed. She opened the door and begrudgingly welcomed me in.

She was dressed only in her bathrobe. She sat back on the bed and resumed brushing her hair with half a dozen brushes.

"I suppose I shouldn't be surprised you found me," she said haughtily.

"You shouldn't be surprised when a private detective finds you," I said. "But you didn't expect us to be good at our jobs. That's why you tried to play us for fools."

"I never played you for fools," she said.

"You played one of us for fools, and now he's doing a doggie paddle down at the docks with a few ounces of lead in him."

"I had a legitimate problem," she said insistently.

"Yes, to find the copy of the Pnakotic Manuscripts, which is quite different from the Silver Key."

She paused her hair brushing. "Oh."

"So don't give me some crap about having a legitimate problem. You were trying to sell us a sucker story since the moment your heels clicked through the door."

"Then why are you here?"

"Who killed Dagon?"

"I don't know," she said simply.

"Tell me another one, sister," I said. "You lure him out, crash an illicit deal, he makes off with the goods, and you don't know what happened?"

"Everything went bad," she said. "I lost track of him in the chaos."

"Everyone wants what he had, yet everyone lost track of him until he dies," I said. "Something stinks here."

"I'm telling the truth," she said.

I sighed and rubbed my head. I looked over to the minibar where she had quite the selection of liquor. I was suddenly thirsty. But I was not about to turn my back on her.

"Make me a drink, sweetheart," I said.

She rolled her eyes but stood up and went to the minibar. As she fixed the drink, she turned her head to look at me. "This stuff will kill you, y'know."

"I choose to take that risk," I said as she handed me the drink.

"Let's go over the evening, shall we? Tell me everything that happened." I took a sip of my drink. I felt calmer.

She sighed dramatically and laid down on the bed. Her legs were up and sticking out of the folds of her robe, making sure I got a good look at them. "Dagon met me at Club KIY. We had drinks and talked about the auction. He said he'd help me get it back. However, he said he thought someone was listening - he didn't tell me who. We took the back exit. Some men tried to stop us, but Dagon punched one of them and he escaped."

"A nightgaunt, right?" I said.

She shook her head slowly and pursed a few of her lips. "No, these were masked men. And not cultist trash. They had yellow masks."

"Masks?" That sounded familiar.

"Yeah, they were thugs, but I don't think they were Azathoth's."

"Go on, what about after that?"

"We took a cab to the warehouse," she said. "That's where the auction was. We arrived and I put in my bid for it. There was some conflict within the auction. There was shouting and then there was shooting. Dagon and I were separated in the chaos. I looked for him, but I couldn't find him. So I came back here and locked the door. I heard about his death this morning."

"Auction, huh? I heard that it was just a deal and that you were neither buyer nor seller."

She tossed her hair haughtily. "Such closed minded ideas. Until things change hands, a transaction is always open to other offers. That's the free market."

"I get the feeling that this particular market was not intended to be free," I said. My eyes were feeling heavy. It had been one very long day.

"That's not something I care about. If I want something, I get it. Secrecy is someone else's problem."

"I'm sure they felt the same way, and that's why they started shooting," I said with a sigh. Dealing with Old Ones was sometimes like dealing with children. Vastly intelligent and unfathomly powerful children from spaces beyond the comprehension of the human reach with appetites that consumed worlds and surrounded by large organizations of cultists willing to die to serve their wills, but children nonetheless. Some days I wonder if I'd be better off on another pantheon.

She shrugged. "That's the last time I saw Dagon."

"Where is the Silver Key?"

She laughed, a tinkling sound like a madman playing a xylophone in a hall of mirrors. "I thought *you* had it! I was going to come visit you tonight in something slinky to find out. You've saved me the trouble of getting dressed." I looked over to a red dressed laid out on the bed. It was the type of dress that women poured themselves into so that they oozed sex out of every available pore. She would have looked damn good in it.

"Who else was at the auction?" I noticed a strange stutter in my voice. I was feeling really tired suddenly. Almost dizzy.

She simply looked at me expectantly with a smile spread across all her mouths.

"Who else was there?" I said again, more forcefully. The room was beginning to spin.

I looked down at the glass in my hand as it wobbled and fell out of my shaking claws. Drugged! She had slipped me a mickey! I looked over to Shub-Niggurath and noticed her self-satisfied smile. That was the last thing I saw before I blacked out.

7

When I next opened my eyes, I was in a swank office full of antiques. Before me was a large wooden desk with a phone, some notebooks, and various curios from the Near East. On the other side was the vast bulk of a toad smoking a hookah. He wore a red fez and a white suit that he had very obviously sweated through. He had a very gentile attitude, though I knew he was as dangerous as any other Old One, maybe more so.

"I see you are awake, Mr. Cthulhu," he said in a rich baritone marred only by his thick frog lips and the shriek of madmen in a thousand universes.

"I'll admit that I didn't suspect you were involved, Tsathoggua," I said. I found I was in a red cushioned armchair. I wasn't tied or restrained, but I noticed my movements were still slow and heavy. My head throbbed. I no longer had Yog-Sothoth's revolver. I turned around me, checking my exits, and saw the giant lizard Bokrug leaning against the door, a gun held lazily in his hands. That explained who he was working for.

"I'll take that as a compliment," the frog said, grinning around the hookah he held in his mouth with large teeth.

"Of course, since there was the unnamed buyer, it makes sense. *You* were buying the Silver Key and Yog-Sothoth was authenticating the goods - assuming he didn't find a way to get his sweaty palms on it when you weren't looking."

"All correct," he said jovially. "I see you've earned your reputation as a detective, Mr. Cthulhu."

"What I don't get is if Shub-Niggurath drugged me, why am I here? She messed up your deal and tried to buy it out from under you. I would think you two would be enemies."

"Very true!" he said with a laugh. "In that way you were a peace offering, to smooth over all the unpleasantness between us. I've been wanting to meet you and she knew it."

"I have an office, you were always welcome to come by," I said.

"A man like me isn't one to call upon a gentleman at his office," he said. "The world comes to me!" He laughed.

"And just what is it that you've been wanting to see me about?"

"Oh, Mr. Cthulhu, I'm sure you know what I'm after. The Silver Key!"

"Everybody's after the damn thing," I said.

"As well they should!" said the fat toad enthusiastically. "In his disappearance, the man known as Randolph Carter has left behind something fantastic. A key to a gate we are unable to open. A back door! The Key is the means to accelerating any of our plans! Of course we all want it, but I will be the one to have it, Mr. Cthulhu."

He was an enthusiastic madman, but still a madman. "That's great," I said, "so what do you want with me?"

"Of course I brought you here to discuss the whereabouts of the Silver Key."

"I don't have it," I said, "and if you're asking me, then you don't have it either. Pretty short discussion."

He laughed softly. "Oh Mr. Cthulhu, one does not get to my position in life by just trusting people at face value. Your partner, Mr. Dagon, absconded with it. It was not found on his corpse. So of course, all those facts would lead someone right to your door."

"You're welcome to search the place - or you would have been, if Yog-Sothoth had not done it already."

"Yes. Well, certain individuals have been a little more... shall we say *enthusiastic* in searching for the Key."

"I can tell you that my office does not appreciate his enthusiasm."

He chuckled. "Oh, Mr. Cthulhu you are a card! But we already knew that the Key did not reside at your office."

"And you had some of your goons pat me down when you brought me here, right?" My clothes felt like they weren't on properly, causing me to shift uncomfortably in the chair.

"Just so, Mr. Cthulhu. And as we've been talking, my cultists are currently in your apartment searching for the Key."

"I knew there was a reason you were being so friendly and long winded," I said.

"Nonsense, Mr. Cthulhu! The world seems to have forgotten pleasantries and manners," said the man who had my drugged body brought to his office. "Though if you wanted to leave here before my men finished their search, I'd have to object."

"Great, so I'm a prisoner."

"Oh, don't think of it that way, Mr. Cthulhu. We're just having a long talk. Would you care for some tea or brandy?"

"You can keep your tea along with your pleasantries. After my last drink, I find myself not thirsty."

He chuckled again. "Ho ho, Mr. Cthulhu! I see your wit is never lacking!"

I shifted in my chair. My head still throbbed like a stampede of Mi-Go were racing back and forth in it. I couldn't tell if it was from the drug Shub-Niggurath slipped me or from the fall to her floor. "So tell me, Tsathoggua, who killed Dagon?"

"That's quite a change in subject, Mr. Cthulhu. I believe I was asking *you* the questions."

"You have only one question and that's do I know where the Silver Key is," I said. "I don't. Even if you think I'm lying, you're not going to get a different answer out of me. So you might as well indulge my questions."

"Just so, Mr. Cthulhu, just so! At least we have no illusions between us and you have described our situation quite eloquently. The only truly honest thing I could say is that I did not personally kill Mr. Dagon, nor did I give the order to any of my men to do it."

"Well, thank you for being honest," I said sarcastically.

"I owed the man no ill will," said Tsathoggua. "It has all been business for me. After the unpleasantness at the deal, Mr. Yog-Sothoth, Mr. Bokrug, and I searched for both Mr. Dagon and Ms. Shub-Niggurath all night, but unfortunately we found neither. It was not until the police found the body did I realize that your poor partner was deceased."

"And I'm sure Yog-Sothoth will gladly confirm your alibi," I said sourly.

"As well he should, as I spent all night with the sniveling fool as he claimed exclusive knowledge and sorcery which failed to find either one of our quarry. He is a sometimes needed associate, but I am glad when I do not need to call upon him."

"Great," I said. "Dagon buys the farm and the three bullets in his back manage to not be anybody's fault."

"I sympathize with your dilemma, Mr. Cthulhu, but that is all that I know."

The phone on Tsathoggua's desk rang. He picked it up and listened. Then he examined me while nodding. Then he said yes a few times before hanging it up.

"You are free to go," he said simply. I heard the slithering bulk of Bokrug move away from the door.

"Didn't find anything at my apartment, did you?" I said.

He simply smiled. "Goodbye, Mr. Cthulhu."

8

Leaving Tsathoggua's office in the back of N'kai Imports, I discovered it was morning. I hoped that while drugged I got a good night's sleep as I didn't have time for it now. I knew my apartment had been ransacked, but I first wondered about Dagon's apartment. I lived alone, but Dagon had a wife.

Mother Hydra, Dagon's wife, was a mess. Her eyes were dark from crying. She wore only a robe. The place was in shambles.

She gave me a far too intimate hug, but I didn't say anything. Her husband had just been killed.

"They came in the middle of the night," she said with tears. "They had guns... Cthulhu, were they the ones who killed Dagon?"

"At this point, I don't know. Here, sit down and tell me about them." I gently directed her towards a kitchen chair that hadn't been overturned and I began making coffee. We could both use a cup of joe.

"Most of them were just black dripping shapes trying to mimic men," she said distastefully.

"Formless spawn," I said with a nod. Tsathoggua's people.

"But they were being directed by a big lizard in a suit," she said. "He sat me down on the couch and sat across from me, a gun in his hand, and just watched me until they finished. He never blinked."

Bokrug. I had just seen him at Tsathoggua's, so there was no doubt who had done this. I guessed the Formless Spawn searched here first before heading over to my apartment.

"Did they say anything?" I asked.

"Not the shapes, but the lizard kept asking me where 'the key' was. I showed him the key to the front door, but I don't think that's what he wanted. He just stared at me." She wiped her tears as I put down a cup of coffee in front of her. "Cthulhu, just what was Dagon involved in?"

"I'm still trying to find out," I said. "But I need you to answer some questions. Did he come home the other night? Did he give you anything?"

She shook her heads. "He called just before dinner to say he was working a case and was going to be out late." She noticed my sigh and paused. "Was there no case?"

I chose my words carefully. "I turned down a case, but he decided to take it on his own. He didn't tell me about it."

She frowned, close to tears again. "He never came home. I waited up, but eventually I fell asleep. He called and woke me up in the middle of the night. I couldn't hear him well, but he said something went bad. He said he couldn't get in touch with you. I think someone was after him. He just said something about meeting at the docks. Then the line went dead." She began crying.

Now I frowned. He must have tried to contact me, but I was passed out at the office and not at home. But who was he meeting at the docks? His body was found there, so that was his final destination. But had he hit the docks twice for some reason, before the deal and after? That seemed unlikely. I think this confirmed he made it out of the deal alive. But where was the Silver Key?

"Hydra, listen," I said, grabbing her arms and trying to calm her down, "did he tell you anything more? Did he say anything about a book or a key?"

She sadly shook her head. I sighed. I told her I'd be in touch, but I had things to do and doubted I'd get back to her any time soon. I needed to find the Silver Key. I knew that would help me find out who killed him.

Little did I know that it would find me.

9

Returning home, I found my apartment trashed. It almost seemed malicious how much was destroyed and overturned. Worse, there were wet black handprints over everything. I cleared enough away from the bed to lay down just to rest for a moment. Before I knew it, I was waking up at noon. A quick shower and I was on my way.

I returned to my office mid-afternoon. I had a bunch of new information, but little in the way of leads. Everyone wanted the Silver Key but nobody knew what Dagon did with it. I was no closer to finding his killer. I had plenty of suspects but no smoking gun. I needed someone for the police or I'd be taking the fall for his murder.

Bokrug was watching my office. That was obvious to anyone. There was no use in trying to hide his bulk and he didn't try. He simply watched me enter the building in his typical unblinking expressionless manner.

I bumped into the parcel carrier in the lobby. In addition to bills, he had a package for me. It was a lumpy thing wrapped in brown paper and tied with string. My name and address had been written on it in a shaky hand. I thought about Bokrug across the street and wondered if I hadn't met the carrier whether my package would have still been here.

Stuffing the package under my coat, I made my way up to my office, hoping to avoid any other interested observers. Once inside, I put the package on my desk and used my claws to cut the string open. Inside the package was a book bound in leather - its binding old, the pages thick and uneven. On top of the book was a note. The note was brief, the handwriting shaky, but it was Dagon's.

DEAL WENT BAD. MEETING AT DOCKS. KEEP THIS SAFE.

This confirmed some of what I heard. But who was he meeting at the docks? Right now, that was likely his killer.

The cover of the book indicated it was the Pnakotic Manuscripts, but I knew this had to be a fake or recent reproduction. The book had never looked so shabby any of the times I had seen the known copies. I opened the book and found that it wasn't truly a book. The pages inside were the printed text of some author known as Lovecraft, but it was obvious this wasn't intended to be read. A depression had been carved into the page. In this depression laid the Silver Key.

For all the talk about it, the Silver Key wasn't very impressive. Yes, it was silvery and picked up the light when you turned it in your hand, but it probably was not actually silver. It was an old key made for a lock that didn't technically exist. If the reputation was true, it would open the gate of dreams... and a fair amount of other things. Any Old One could use that as a new avenue for taking over Earth or any of the other mortal realms. But up close, it just looked like any old key that someone had slapped a coat of silver paint on.

Though I had my doubts to its authenticity, that was unimportant. Whether it had any inherent worth, everyone wanted it, so it was priceless. I could use it to bargain for Dagon's killer and probably much more. If I lived that long.

By this point, I knew that anyone watching my office had seen both parcel carrier and I enter. While I didn't expect Bokrug to be smart enough to put the two together, I would be shocked if he was the only one staking out my office. Someone else that was watching was going to connect the carrier and I. That meant I needed to get the Silver Key to a safe place. But I knew if I walked out the front with it, I'd have at least one tail.

The building my office is in doesn't actually have a back door; all deliveries and utility services are through the front. But there is a window on the second floor hallway that faces the back alley. I had never used it, though Dagon had used it a few times when his wife had shown up unexpectedly.

As I slid out that somewhat tight window, I realized that I had forgotten that it opened about fifteen feet off the ground. I fell down on the dumpster below it then eased myself off that onto the ground. It could have been a worse fall, but I knew I'd be carrying the lingering smell of this place for a few hours at least.

I got halfway down the alley toward the street before someone jumped me. He came running down the alley carrying a baseball bat. I'm guessing that he eschewed a gun in case they needed to question me. Still, a baseball bat was better than my bare claws. I noticed that he was wearing a mask.

I didn't have any space to run. I lucked out that in his rabid charge, he slipped on a garbage bag and came stumbling towards me. I used that opportunity to step inside his swinging range, hoping to be too close for him to properly strike me.

Unfortunately, he still managed to swing the bat upwards. Since I was so close, it turned a major concussion into just a dizzying hit. I admit I saw stars that weren't right in my blurry vision. But that didn't stop me from linking my claws together and slamming them down together on the back of my assailant's neck. He fell to the ground limply.

I noticed that blood had begun to drip from my forehead. I grabbed my handkerchief and wiped it up. I probably had a helluva bruise too.

I didn't have time to search him, since I expected he would not have been the only one to notice my attempted escape. I did take a moment to stare at the mask. It was a full face mask, but it was divided down the center, making it appear to be two masks put together. One half was in the style of the old thespian masks where one is sad and one is happy. Instead of happy, this one seemed to have a frenzied madness, the smile too wide, the eyes too sharply carved. The other half of the mask was a blank white, featureless expect for a generic eyehole. The mad half of the mask was a bright yellow.

A yellow thespian mask. This had to be one of Johnny Hastur's men. What was his interest in all this? Was he at the supposed auction?

I trotted quickly to the end of the alley and opened a gate where there was room. I didn't use the gate to head home or to some strange other dimension. No, I took it to the R'lyeh bus station.

Rewrapping it in brown paper and string, I left the Silver Key in the fake Pnakotic Manuscripts and stashed that in a bus station locker. I put the locker key in my pocket. Perhaps I should have been amused at the idea of carrying a key to the Key, but at the time my mind was devising a plan with grim determination. I finally had the one thing everyone wanted. I could use it myself, but that wasn't worthwhile if I still had Dagon's murder pinned on me. I could sell it, but again, without someone taking the fall for Dagon, I would not be able to enjoy my newfound wealth. I needed to find his killer.

I took a gate back to my office. I checked the alley first for Hastur's henchman, since I now had the time to search him properly, but the alley was empty. I considered climbing back through the window to enter the office that way, but I'm pretty sure that would fool only Bokrug. I turned back toward the street, intending to head around to the front entrance.

Instead, someone stepped out in front of the exit. I saw their silhouette against the light and knew who it was immediately. I heard the clack of heels down the alley toward me. She had worn the red dress this time, I saw appreciatively. She also carried a gun.

I realized that I needed to spend less time in alleys. They were never good for my health.

10

"Where is it?" said Shub-Niggurath.

"Don't have it," I said.

She laughed tensely. "That excuse worked before, but we know you have it now."

"We?" I said. "I thought you were working alone. Well, except when you worked with Dagon and got him killed."

"We have decided to put aside our differences to get the Key," she said. "Then we can all use it to invade the Earth realm."

"That must feel nice," I said. "All the suckers lined up in front of you with their backs ready for you to stab when the stars are right. Thing is, what's going to happen when it's your neck that's stuck out?"

"I assure you I can take care of myself," she said.

"Or find someone to take care of you," I said. "Someone easily discarded, like Dagon."

"Nobody cares about Dagon," she said.

"I do," I said. "I'm not going up the river for something I didn't do."

"If you keep being difficult, you won't have to worry about that," she said, gesturing with the gun and moving closer.

"What's Johnny Hastur's stake in all this?" I asked.

Her brow furrowed in confusion. "What? He's not part of -"

I took her confusion to make my move. I grabbed her hand with the gun and slammed it into the alley wall. The gun dropped. I gave her a push. She stumbled on her heels and fell into some trash.

I leaned down and grabbed the gun. I checked the cylinder. Three bullets left, three empty. By the scent, the gun had been fired recently.

"This dress is ruined now," she said, taking off her heels so she could pull herself up. There was a stain on the rear of her dress. I didn't want to think what she fell in.

I pointed the gun at her again.

"You don't need that to threaten me," she said distastefully, "the threat of pushing me into more garbage is enough to make me more cooperative." She put her heels back on, giving a frustrated cluck when she found one of the heels had broken. She tossed that into a pile of garbage.

"What's Hastur's role in all this?" I said.

She shrugged. "He wasn't invited to the auction, though he tried to crash it. He was never part of negotiations. None of us wanted him involved."

"Who's us? Who's your new alliance?"

"Tsathoggua, Yog-Sothoth and myself," she said.

"That's quite an alliance," I said. "Are you sure you trust Tsathoggua?"

"Truth be told," she said, trying to smooth her dress, "Tsathoggua originally hired Yog-Sothoth and I to help get the Key. We just ended up wanting it for ourselves. So I think you might be better off giving him the speech about trust."

"I want to meet with them," I said.

"To push them into trash and ruin their dresses?" she suggested.

"To make a deal," I said.

11

Shub-Niggurath and I headed back to her seedy hotel room. Despite her admission, I kept the gun on her the whole time from my jacket pocket. We went to her hotel because I didn't want to meet at Tsathoggua's office or wherever the hell Yog-Sothoth worked out of. I wanted the home field advantage and the element of surprise.

She called them and asked them to come to her room. She said it was urgent. She said she knew where the Key was. It took some repeating, but eventually she managed to even get Tsathoggua to leave his office. She didn't mention me at all, as I instructed, but with all her lies and games, I wouldn't have put it past her to have some code that alerted her allies. Then again, she didn't seem the type to do favors for even her allies.

When they showed up, I hid behind the door, Shub-Niggurath's gun in my hand. First was the nervous form of Yog-Sothoth. He had a bandage on his head sphere where I had cracked it. Next was the wide sweaty bulk of Tsathoggua himself, looking reluctant to have left the safety of his office. Lastly came the unmistakable bulk of Bokrug, his suit still ill-fitting and bulging.

After Bokrug passed by, I slammed the door closed and made sure they all saw the gun in my hand. Bokrug had immediately tensed, but I shook the gun at him. He backed off and slid into the corner. Yog-Sothoth swallowed nervously.

Tsathoggua laughed. "Well done, Mr. Cthulhu! I hardly expected to find you here, much less taking the advantage!"

"Cut the crap," I said. "I have the Silver Key now and I'm willing to make a deal."

There was a pause as this set in. A few looks were shared.

"I am very interested in making that deal," said Tsathoggua, elated. "What are your terms?"

"First off, I want a hundred grand," I said.

There was a gasp from Shub-Niggurath and Yog-Sothoth went wide eyed. Tsathoggua waved them both off with his hand. "That's quite a high price," said Tsathoggua.

"True," I said, "but we all know it's worth far more than that."

"Naturally," he said. "I believe we can make that work." The others looked unsure, but I knew that this was mostly Tsathoggua's deal. Their alliance might fall apart soon. "What are your other terms?"

"Someone's gotta take the fall for killing Dagon," I said.

This provoked a much more emotional reaction. It was amusing to watch their true natures come out, their double dealing, their survival instincts. I knew very well that I had backed them into a corner and someone was going to be sacrificed.

They began whispering. They knew that for it to stick, it had to be one of them. They couldn't finger some random stranger. I wondered if up until now they had intended on letting me go down on that rap. I chuckled a moment later. Of course that was their plan - right up until I had the Silver Key and a gun on them.

After a few minutes of terse conversation, recriminations, and low voices on the other side of the room, they had an answer. Tsathoggua, as if representative for them all, cleared his throat. "Ahem, we have decided that Bokrug shall take responsibility for that crime."

I turned and looked at Bokrug. For once his expressionless reptile face had an expression: shock. Obviously this hadn't been cleared with him.

"Don't worry about it," said Tsathoggua. "You're young. You'll be out of prison in no time and still have plenty of time to devour civilizations!"

Bokrug did not see it the same way. He growled. I aimed the gun at him, wondering what he might do. For a split second, I wondered if he was going to turn on Tsathoggua and tear him apart. Instead, with a sharp cry, he barreled past me and out the door of the room. I let him go; I didn't want to shoot him if we were going to pin a murder on him. And I wasn't about to grapple with that behemoth while holding the gun. It would be too easy for him to grab the gun and I would lose everything I had gained.

We all watched Bokrug trot down the length of the hall before I closed the door.

"Don't worry about him," said Tsathoggua. "Between us all we have enough testimony to incriminate him with the Elder Gods even if he doesn't confess."

"I never liked him anyway," said Yog-Sothoth. "He never seemed canonical."

"Now, do you have any other terms?" said Tsathoggua.

"I shouldn't have to say that you don't incriminate me at all," I said, "but with this bunch, I might as well make sure it is on the table. I come out of this clean."

"Of course, Mr. Cthulhu," said Tsathoggua, "what do you take us for?"

I simply gave him a look. "A bunch of untrustworthy Old Ones who would sell every single last cultist they had down the river if they thought it would give them an advantage when the stars were right."

Tsathoggua chuckled. "Just so, Mr. Cthulhu, just so!"

I rolled my eyes. "So what about the money?"

"I can give you ten grand now," said Tsathoggua, "and the remainder when you bring the Key to my office."

"Your office?" balked Shub-Niggurath. If earlier wasn't a sign, she now realized this was rapidly changing from Their Deal to Tsathoggua's Deal.

The fat toad paused and looked at Yog-Sothoth and Shub-Niggurath. "Unless one of you can help with the down payment?" Both of them suddenly found something else to look at rather than meet his gaze. "As I suspected."

"Fine, I'll meet you there in an hour," I said, moving toward the door.

"Wait," said Tsathoggua. He looked almost embarrassed. "It's not that I don't trust you, but..."

"But you don't trust me," I said.

"Just so," he said. "I would like to send a representative with you."

"Who?" I asked. "How do I know you're not going to have them jump me and steal the Key?"

"Well, since we no longer have Mr. Bokrug..." He looked to his companions. "Then maybe Ms. Shub - " he stopped himself. "No, that won't do. Yog-Sothoth. Would you accompany Mr. Cthulhu?"

Yog-Sothoth smiled weakly.

"Unarmed," I said.

"What?" said Tsathoggua.

"He's going to have to be unarmed," I said. "I already have the Key and I already have the jump on you now. If I was going to double cross you I would have done it already. And I need you to incriminate Bokrug. Unarmed means he or you can't double-cross *me*."

"I suppose I will have to agree with your logic," said Tsathoggua. He turned to Yog-Sothoth. "Give me your pistol." Yog-Sothoth seemed reluctant, but Tsathoggua turned up the heat. "You've already lost it once, you'll probably lose it again."

Yog-Sothoth reluctantly handed over his revolver.

"Okay, I'll see you at your office in an hour," I said.

That meeting never happened.

12

Yog-Sothoth and I took a gate to the bus station. He seemed amused by the location as I walked over to the lockers. Then the smiles left both our faces as we saw the damage.

Someone had wrenched the lockers open. It wasn't just mine open, but all of them. The book and the key were missing from my locker. On the edge of mine was a piece of fabric that had torn on a twisted corner. It was yellow silk. Hastur.

"Why does Hastur want the Key?" I asked Yog-Sothoth.

He said nothing, his thin lips tensed.

"Come on, this benefits both of us. You can give out free information," I said.

"Hastur wants the Key for his play," he said.

That damn play again. "Why? Why would he want the Silver Key for it?"

Yog-Sothoth grimaced. "So that the play can unmake all of reality."

13

We decided to head over to N'kai Imports to meet Tsathoggua. We didn't have the Key, but we had bigger fish to fry. If Hastur could unmake reality, it would put a wrench in all our plans. We didn't want reality simply wiped away. At the very least we each hoped we could rend and devour reality ourselves rather than have it pulled out from under us. We knew that Tsathoggua and Shub-Niggurath would feel the same and lend us some aid.

As we arrived at the street for N'kai Imports, Yog-Sothoth saved me. I was shocked he did it, but I was grateful. As I started walking forward, Yog-Sothoth grabbed my arm and pulled me into the shadow of an alley.

I had not noticed it at first, but the front of N'kai Imports was swarming with police. Uniformed Hounds of Tindalos were all over and I saw a few Elder Gods in plainclothes. As we watched, we saw them pull out a body on a stretcher.

"Tsathoggua," said Yog-Sothoth glumly.

I looked closer. He was right. That was definitely the fat toad in his white suit. It looked like he had been gored and shredded by some very sharp teeth.

They then pulled out another body, even more enormous than Tsathoggua's. The gargantuan reptile corpse was even more obvious. Bokrug. Bullet holes riddled that scaly flesh.

Yog-Sothoth and I looked at each other.

So much of our plan just went up in smoke. We couldn't pin Dagon's murder on either of them without opening it up to the whole Key situation. Yog-Sothoth correctly guessed when he dragged me into the shadows: we didn't want to be persons of interest in the N'kai murders. Just being seen by the police would be problematic. The help we had hoped to get for hitting Hastur and getting the Key back was also gone.

We looked to see if Shub-Niggurath was in the back of a squad car or lingering in the area but did not see her. We weren't surprised; we expected she had fled at the first sign of trouble. We took a gate to her hotel room but found it empty, her belongings cleared out. She had either left town or gone to ground.

We looked at each other grimly. We both knew that Hastur had to be stopped; running was not an option. We also knew we were going in woefully unprepared.

14

The front of Club KIY buzzed with activity. There were new signs announcing a special enhanced showing of that damned play, *The King in Yellow*. The rich socialites were actually out in droves tonight, the front clogged with limos. Who knew that all you needed to pull in the rich dilettantes was an art production that ends all of reality?

Of course, it wasn't just socialites that were filling the front of Club KIY. There were also quite a few of Azathoth's thugs working security. The rich socialites seemed okay with heavily muscled and heavily armed men as long as they were keeping the peace. I wasn't sure if Azathoth was in on it with Hastur or if Johnny Hastur had merely spent the money for the best non-legal security he could buy. The latter seemed more likely.

The front was a no-go. I'm pretty sure that Hastur would have my name on a list of people to watch out for. He had stolen the Silver Key right out of my locker. I also bet that he had Yog-Sothoth on that list just as good practice, even if he didn't know Yog-Sothoth was involved. He's not the type you want wandering around when you make your big move.

Luckily, I knew about the back alley from the last time I was at the club. Of course, Hastur knew that I knew about the alley too, so it was unfortunately guarded. It was only guarded by one thug, but he was carrying a Tommy gun.

Yog-Sothoth was unarmed, his pistol left at Tsathoggua's. I still had Shub-Niggurath's revolver, but it only had three bullets. Unfortunately that didn't really qualify me to get in a shooting match with a thug wielding a Tommy gun. Also, I'd rather not have anyone fire, since the sound would alert everyone inside the club. I was pretty sure that this wouldn't be the only Tommy gun.

I decided that sneaking would be the best plan. It was night and there were enough trash and bins in the long alley that I felt like we could make it up to the open area behind the club. The thug was bored. He smoked a cigarette and paced back and forth, almost never looking down the alley. I'm sure to him the idea of someone trying to sneak in the back past a guy with a Tommy gun was ludicrous.

Secure in our ludicrous plan, we slowly crept forward. I noticed that the Deep One corpse I had seen yesterday was gone. Someone had taken that away, but I wasn't sure who. All in all, it took us about five minutes to slowly and agonizingly creep to the opening near the back of the club. The thug paced back and forth about ten feet away.

We were crouched behind a half wall created by trash cans. We peered over at the armed thug. I turned to Yog-Sothoth and inclined my head towards the thug. Yog-Sothoth shook his head sphere "no" vigorously. I sighed and realized I was on my own.

The thug was walking back and forth, almost like clockwork. He had smoked at least two cigarettes over the time we had crept into the alley and hid behind the trashcans and he showed no sign of stopping. Assuming he would continue this bizarre repetitive behavior, I was going to wait until he passed us, then quickly sneak out and hit him on the back of his head.

He swung past us, his cigarette burned down to halfway. I slipped out from behind the trash cans. Light on my feet, I took a step towards him, then another. I was eager to just rush forward and hit him, but if I moved too quickly, then he'd hear me and turn around. But if I moved too slowly, he'd reach the end of his pacing and turn around and see me anyway. So I tried to balance speed and silence. I was succeeding in my stealth and I was almost behind him. I raised my arm to strike and -

A trash can lid clattered down to the ground. Yog-Sothoth had leaned too hard on the trash can. He looked at us sheepishly. I looked over to the guard who had turned to look at Yog-Sothoth and now saw me.

I lunged forward and grabbed at the Tommy gun as the thug dropped his cigarette and tried to raise the gun. I was holding it with both hands, pushing it down towards his leg as he was trying to force it upward. There was grunting, but as long as he didn't pull the trigger, it wouldn't make enough noise to alert anyone inside.

While I had the leverage of pushing down, I was beginning to realize that the thug was stronger than me. Azathoth tended to hire his thugs a certain way: big, dumb, stupid, and okay with the insanity of an ever-expanding indifferent void where everything will end in a cold, lonely death. The thug was gaining on me, raising the gun slowly.

We struggled for thirty seconds, but it seemed much longer than that. The gun inched up slowly towards my legs. If he got it pointed at my leg and pulled the trigger, this would be all over fast and I'd walk with a permanent limp, assuming he didn't kill me seconds later. I looked to his face, inches away from me as he grunted from the exertion. I realized then what I needed to do.

Leaning forward, my face moved even closer to his. My face tentacles reached out and grasped his forehead. Digging into his skull, it was over. No matter how resistant they might be to Azathoth's madness, there was no defense once I had dug my tentacles into their mind.

His grip released immediately and I ripped the Tommy gun from him. His eyes glazed over and he fell to his knees. His bottom lip shivered and white foamy drool began to pour from his mouth. A few seconds later and I had devoured his mind, leaving him an empty shell of a man, too feeble to even whisper his own name in the dark.

I tapped him gently and he fell over to the ground. I grabbed a satchel with extra bullet cartridges that he had left against the wall.

Yog-Sothoth came out from behind the garbage cans. "Sorry," he said with a wincing smile.

I ignored him and checked the Tommy gun. I rolled my eyes when I saw that the safety was still on. I clicked it off and held it with both hands.

"We have a play to cancel," I said.

15

The inside of Club KIY was dark, the play already in progress. Due to the darkness, we made our way inside unnoticed. The stage was lit by an amber light, while men in masks pantomimed activity. Occasionally one of them said some pithy line about the state of the universe, but otherwise it seemed pretty boring. Most of them wore masks like my assailant in my office's alley: half a yellow face, half blank. But one had a different mask. On the stage there was a wooden throne. On that throne sat a single figure in a yellow silk mask which completely covered their face.

In the stage light I could see out into the sea of patrons. Most were at round tables with white tablecloths. Most men were in tuxedos while the women were in a variety of fancy dresses. That confirmed Hastur had finally truly attracted his favored clientele: the idle rich. I guess that was fitting for the day which he expected to be his greatest success. I was here to make sure it would be his greatest failure.

Indoor security was much less tight than it was outside. I'm sure that Hastur didn't like the idea of Azathoth's grunts clomping around his club or his stage production. Yog-Sothoth and I were easily able to make our way to the backstage area, passing worried actors and enthralled cultists. One of Azathoth's thugs did notice me, but he waved me past. In the darkness, all he saw was a man holding a Tommy gun, so he must have assumed I was one of theirs.

From the wings we could see the stage production. There were more actors with yellow masks and more bizarre stage props that they were running onto the stage. I didn't see Johnny Hastur, but I wouldn't have put it past him to be the figure on the throne. We needed to focus on finding the key.

Luck was with us. I overheard from the stage:

"This gate will unmake the universe! The door will open, reality will be inverted, and we will be left alone. All alone!"

"But why must we endure such woe?"

"Because we must! Because we must! Bring the key!"

My opinions on Hastur's lyrical ability are the matter of public record, so I will not talk further on that point here. But right after this was said, I noticed an actor walk right past me. He wore the half yellow mask, but what was important was what was in his hands. He held that fake version of the Pnakotic Manuscripts, the cover open so that the Silver Key could be seen. He held the book open and with the palms of his hands at heart level, as if it were a religious item. He walked slowly, left foot, right foot, as if in a march.

I grabbed his shoulder and yanked him backwards. He resisted at first. Unfortunately he was halfway onto the stage when I did this, so it was visible to everyone - actors, audience, security. The audience and the security out near the tables didn't know that this wasn't part of the show, but the actors did, and there was a sudden murmuring from them. I yanked harder on the actor's shoulder and he tumbled back toward me, the book toppling to the ground.

Yog-Sothoth dove for the book. The king on the throne gestured toward me. The actors began howling and ran at me. The audience was still confused. Security stared on but didn't move yet. I raised the Tommy gun towards the actors, but that threat did nothing. They still ran toward me with malicious intent and were unafraid of the stream of bullets I was about to unleash.

I had known this was going to be inevitable. I opened fire with the Tommy gun. The muzzle flashed and the barrel roared. It kicked like a mule and I used all my strength to keep it steady as it mowed down a steady stream of Hastur's actors. I sprayed the stage, even catching those actors that didn't immediately come at me.

I *may* have laughed maniacally while I did this.

While I fired, Yog-Sothoth had pulled the Key from the book with great excitement, holding it up triumphantly. "At last! The Key! The Silver Key!"

I was shocked that this didn't make him a target, but he was largely ignored. He set to work verifying the authenticity of the Key in the middle of a shoot out. He's always been a little weird.

By this point, the rest of the club was chaos. The audience of rich socialites were screaming and making a bum rush for the door. This actually was to my benefit for the first moments of the fight, as they swarmed around security, who weren't able to get a clear shot at me. But that didn't last long. Azathoth's thugs finally began firing at me with their own Tommy guns.

I found myself taking cover behind the throne. The king with the yellow silk mask was still in the chair, having been sprayed with bullets. He was pretty bloody. The silk mask slipped from his face and confirmed it was Johnny Hastur. He wheezed for breath. "This was supposed to be my greatest... masterpiece..." he gasped.

"Nobody likes your damn play," I said, sliding a new cartridge in my gun. "Nobody has *ever* liked your damn plays. You weren't even a good singer."

I leaned out from behind the throne and started firing. All the still-living members of the audience had now left, leaving me with six of Azathoth's thugs trying to hide between tables that had been turned on their sides. I was glad that Hastur had bought crappy thin tables that did little to stop bullets. Two of the thugs had Tommy guns, but the rest just had pistols.

My shots cut down one of those two thugs with a Tommy gun as the goon next to him dove for a table. At this point we all had cover, so it was a fight of attrition. We'd all dig in until the cops showed up, then we'd all run like hell, hoping our opponents were the ones who got grabbed by the Hounds.

Of course, Yog-Sothoth has always had a great ability at disrupting a perfectly good fight. A howl of sadness erupted from him, loud and tortured enough that even the thugs paused to look at him.

"It's a fake!" he shouted. "It's a fake!"

We all stared at him in shock.

"What?" said Hastur weakly, blood dripping out of his mouth.

"It's not the real Silver Key!" cried Yog-Sothoth. "It's not Randolph Carter's Silver Key! The Dreamer tricked us!"

It was like a great energy was sucked from the room. We all still theoretically wanted to kill each other, but now there felt like there was no point to it. We had been fighting over something that was of vast value. Now we knew we were tricked and were fighting over a piece of cheap dime store trash. The deaths hardly seemed worth it, and I normally love deaths.

In this silence, we heard the first police sirens. The fight might have gone on longer had it not been interrupted, but since we were in this strange lull, we heard the sirens sooner than if guns were blazing. Following some unspoken agreement, Azathoth's thugs filed out of the club, keeping the final Tommy gun carrier covering me. Then he left quickly. They needn't have worried, I was done with this farce.

Yog-Sothoth was in a state of shock. He was still whining about the Key. I tried to get him to come with me as I exited through the back door, but he was nonresponsive. I left him there and exited in the alley. I dropped the Tommy gun in a dumpster and made my exit.

16

They never had the Silver Key. The Dreamer either never had it either or he chose to sell them a fake. They had all thought the Key was in their grasp - Shub-Niggurath, Yog-Sothoth, Hastur, Tsathoggua, maybe even Azathoth. They chased it all foolishly and now half of them were dead. I wanted to wash my hands of all of it.

But there was still one loose end and it was the only loose end that mattered: who killed Dagon? And who was going to swing for it?

I had an idea of who did it; truthfully, I thought I knew for sure who did it. But I lacked proof.

The next morning I sat in my office, knowing that this was the last of my three days. I needed to give the Elder Gods Dagon's killer or they'd pin it on me.

I heard the clicking of her heels down the hallway before I saw her shadow on the door. The letters on the door still said *Cthulhu & Dagon*. I'd have to get that changed.

When she came in, she was as sexy as ever, this time in a green dress. She was here because I had asked her to come. My network of Deep Ones had managed to find her at the new flophouse she was hiding at. Having found her, the Deep Ones delivered a message. It said that I knew where the Dreamer was and that I believed he had the real Silver Key.

It was a complete and utter lie. I didn't know where the Dreamer was and I didn't care about the Silver Key. What I did know was that Shub-Niggurath was the last piece of the puzzle.

Yog-Sothoth had been picked up by the police at Club KIY. I wasn't sure if he was being charged. He had a way of weaseling out of such things by making the right deals.

I had found out what killed Tsathoggua and Bokrug. When Tsathoggua had returned to his office for our meeting, he had found

Bokrug waiting for him. Angry at the betrayal, Bokrug had killed the fat toad with his teeth and claws, quite noisily. He took so long and was so loud that the police were waiting for him when he exited. He tried to run and the police had gunned him down.

Hastur had died in Club KIY. Nothing pointed to Azathoth being involved. His muscle had just been hired by Hastur.

That left Shub-Niggurath. She was the last one alive and free. I had expected her to run. I was surprised to find her still in town.

But she still came to see me. Either she believed my lie or was desperate. It could have been both.

"Thanks for coming," I said politely as she sat down.

"Cut the crap," she said, pulling out a cigarette and putting it into a cigarette holder. I lit it for her and she smoked it nervously. She sat forward, her shoulders hunched, her arms crossed in front of her body. "Where's the Dreamer?"

"Who killed Dagon?" I countered.

She laughed around her cigarette, almost coughing. "Who cares? The man was sleaze. I knew for a fact that he was married, but he still gave me a line about wanting to father my thousand and first young."

"He's still dead because you brought him along," I said.

"I've never thought that you were a sentimentalist," she said. "The Silver Key is what matters."

"I don't care about the Silver Key," I said.

"Then you're a fool," she spat at me.

"Did you kill Dagon?" I said.

She turned sideways, smoking her cigarette and eyeing me sideways out of a multitude of eyes. She said nothing.

"He was meeting you at the docks, wasn't he?" I said. "You had never planned on actually buying the Silver Key; you knew Tsathoggua would outbid you. You had arranged for Dagon to steal the Pnakotic Manuscripts and then meet at the docks. But you didn't count on him examining it and finding the Key, did you?"

"Dagon was too nosey," she said. "He should have just given me the book."

"But he didn't, did he?" I said. "When he showed up at the docks, he didn't have the book or the Key. But he had lots of questions - questions you didn't want to answer. So you killed him!"

"I didn't!" she shrieked.

"But you did!" I countered. "Admit it!"

"You have no proof," she said acidly.

I reached into my drawer and pulled out her revolver. "When I took this from you, it had only three bullets. Three had been fired recently. The police found three bullets in Dagon."

"Circumstantial," she said. "It could have been Yog-Sothoth or Bokrug."

"Yog-Sothoth's gun had never been fired," I said, having examined it myself. "He keeps it oiled but it's never been fired. Bokrug doesn't even use a gun to kill. Besides, Dagon didn't know them or trust them. He told his wife that he was meeting someone at the docks. He would have met someone he knew."

"Maybe he was meeting you," she said.

"He was meeting you! You killed Dagon!"

"I didn't!" she shrieked.

"You did!" I said, raising my voice. I stood up from my chair, pointing the gun at her. "You killed Dagon! Admit it!"

"I did!" she finally admitted, screaming. Tears flowed from her many eyes as her voice grew softer. "I did. But I had to! I had to defend myself! When we met at the docks, he had so many questions. He knew I really wanted the Silver Key. He wanted to blackmail me. He wanted me to... do things for him... to him... in exchange for the Key. And then when I refused, he grabbed me. He tried to force me!"

"Tell me another one, sister," I said. "Dagon had been shot in the back in cold blood. He didn't attack you. He didn't even know it was coming. You shot him because you thought he had the Key on him. And when he didn't, you realized you had screwed up. You realized that I must have it. When you couldn't get it from me directly, you handed me over to Tsathoggua so he wouldn't kill you, so that you still had a chance to get the Key. You played Dagon. You've been playing me. You've been playing all of us this whole time."

"But it's just you and me now," she said excitedly. "We can find the Dreamer and make him tell us where the real Key is!"

"There's no you and me," I said. "I never cared about the Silver Key, I only cared about finding out who killed my partner. I don't know where the Dreamer is, I don't even know who he is. I just wanted to know who really killed Dagon."

She practically spat at me and her features hardened. "If you don't know where the Dreamer is, you're useless to me." She started getting up from her seat and grabbing her purse, despite the gun I had on her.

"I wouldn't do that if I were you," I said, but lowering my gun.

She looked at me in confusion. Then from the corner of the room came the Hounds of Tindalos. They grabbed her arms, fixing her with an unbreakable hold. Next materialized two Elder Gods in detective clothes who had been waiting and listening to the entire conversation. Shub-Niggurath was shrieking, but once they used their elder sign badges on her she quieted.

The shorter Elder God sneered at me and saw to Shub-Niggurath. The taller one nodded to me. "Thanks for your assistance, you're off the hook."

There was no further discussion. They had what they wanted and they hated me. I nodded and they took her away, dissolving through the walls, not even needing a gate.

I slumped back in my chair. Case closed, I guess.

I had lost my partner. I had been drugged, attacked, and shot at. I managed to disrupt a play, shoot a bunch of thugs, and solve a murder. A few of my rivals were now dead. All in all, a good case. An entertaining one. It had passed the time well.

I poured myself a drink and wondered what the next case would bring.

Then I heard the roar of my cultists chanting from beyond space. Another one of their rituals. But this was different. The energy was stronger, the chanting louder, the draw powerful. This felt like it could be The One. I felt each repetition of "Ia!" echoing in my mind.

I smiled.

Around me, I felt R'lyeh rising. The dream was slipping away. The fake trappings of the human world fell away. My detective agency dissolved into non-Euclidian structures of insane angles made of Cyclopean masonry. My suit and tie dissolved and my wings spread out behind me. I could feel the entire city rising from the depths of the oceans to the surface, emerging through the waves to the sky.

Now was the time for me to take my rightful place as ruler and destroyer. Now was the time I had waited for, that my cultists yearned for.

The stars were right.

Public Service Announcement

This novella was a mash up between detective noir and mythos fiction. Both are fantastic genres and I expect most readers to be fans of both. But, on the off chance you were attracted to this novel due to just one of those genres, please indulge me.

For Mythos Fans

You're missing out! I recommend that you check out the works of Dashiell Hammett, Raymond Chandler, and Mickey Spillane. Detective noir (also known as Hardboiled) is one of those genres of American fiction that is often parodied but rarely read (yes, I aware of the irony of this being said at the end of a parody mash up work). If you've never read any of these novels, you're missing out on something unique. Some of the great Bogart films and other movies give you an idea of it, but there's something to be said for reading the stories themselves.

For Detective Noir Fans

First let me say how impressed with you I am for reading all the way through this novella. You have a great affection for weirdness and a high tolerance for strangely spelled multisyllabic names and references to things that are never explained in this story. But if you have found yourself interested in strange stories about vast otherworldly entities with networks of madness-seeking cultists, I suggest the works of HP Lovecraft, Clark Ashton Smith, Robert Bloch, Robert E Howard, August Derleth and many, many, MANY others. The Mythos genre, or Cthulhu Mythos as it is often called, began back in the 1930s, but lives on to this day. There are modern writers still dipping their heels in it, as well as the ideas and characters of the Mythos showing up in board games, comics, movies, video games, music, and more. It is a genre and fandom unto its own and you will be in good company.

A Homeowner's Guide to Interdimensional Portals

1

It's the American dream to be happily married, buy a house, and then settle down to start your family. You want your own castle and homestead, a sanctuary of your own, your safest place to defend against the world. It's such an expected dream that the dangers and drawbacks are overlooked. Nobody tells you about the faults and problems you may end up with when you buy a house. Problems that you are stuck dealing with, that you can't run away from. Problems that will destroy you. Sometimes you end up with an interdimensional portal.

I never asked to have a portal. It just came with the house. It was another headache they don't tell new homeowners. They tell you to look for foundation damage, termites, trees that could fall on your house, or an old HVAC system, but nobody mentions the portals. Termites would have been easier.

I didn't go looking for trouble. I blundered upon the portal accidentally. I was doing yard work. The house had been on the market for a while, so the back needed maintenance even when we first viewed it. After the closing period, the backyard was a jungle. I was trimming some bushes and then cut an errant limb. A huge portion of the bush fell and I cursed. But then I saw it. I didn't know what it was at first. I hadn't recalled seeing it in the final walkthrough before we closed on the house, but the bushes would have obscured it.

"Honey," I asked my wife when I approached her at the kitchen table, reading something on her tablet, "do you recall something shimmering out in the yard?"

"What do you mean?" she asked.

"Something shimmering," I prompted, "Something weird. Do you remember seeing something like that when we did the final walkthrough of the house?"

"Something weird?" she said, maybe a little exasperated at my vagueness, but how better could I describe it? "No, but it was raining that day, so I was paying more attention to the inside of the house. I didn't think the yard would have changed radically from our first viewing."

I nodded. I hadn't paid attention to the outside either. All I had seen was an overgrown yard. It wasn't a big deal when the house itself was the priority. But still... "Can you come out here and look at this?"

She let out a frustrated sigh but then put down her tablet and followed me out to the yard. I showed her the area I had been trimming and the space beyond it where the air was sort of shimmering. It appeared to be an oval disc where everything blurred. Maybe about six feet tall and three feet wide. It just stood there, fixed in space.

"No, I've never seen that before," she said carefully. "Maybe it conveyed with the house?"

"I agree it was probably here before, but what is it?"

"Faulty wiring?" she ventured.

"There are no wires near here," I said.

"Gas leak?" she said. "Is this where the utility easement is?"

I shook my head. "Not according to the survey of the property. This should just be regular yard." I looked over to her. "It's weird to you, right?" I walked a circle around it, closer to the fence. "See this is even more odd. From this side it's not visible at all." I walked back around to the front and crouched in front of the portal. I reached out a hand to touch it.

"Don't do that!" shouted my wife suddenly.

I leapt back immediately. "Why? What happened?"

"Nothing," she said. "We just don't know what it is. We shouldn't touch it."

"What should we do then? It's in our yard!"

"Remember that inspector, the one who walked through the house to check for problems? Call him. He's the one who missed it," she said, turning to walk back to the house. "He'll know what this is."

2

"Yeah, I've seen that before," said the home inspector, nodding to himself.

"Well, what is it?" I prompted.

"We're looking at what some call an interdimensional portal." He was the same inspector we used when we bought the house.

"I... I don't even know what that is," I said. I didn't like showing my lack of knowledge in front of him, even though I had contacted him for his expertise.

"Oh, you know, your typical crack in time and space where quantum entanglement links two very different timespace coordinates together. It's mostly a scifi writer trope, but it does show up every so often in houses. It's typically not a very desirable feature."

"Why would that show up on my property?"

"You get them sometimes, especially in older houses like this one." His tone was nonchalant, as if he were simply talking about termites. "Sometimes you find them in a closet, a wardrobe, or in an attic. Occasionally, like this, they're in the yard. Sometimes they just pop up out of nowhere. Wherever they feel like being." He shrugged.

"Our realtor didn't mention anything about an interdimensional portal," I said.

"Yup," he said, "I'm not surprised. It's not a very common or well known house flaw. Usually the old owner will try to hide the fact it's there. It can really kill a sale."

"But we had you over to inspect the place to make sure there wasn't something like this! That was your job! You were supposed to warn us about crap like this!"

"True, true," he said, scratching his forehead. "Thing is, the housing code don't say nothing about interdimensional portals. I'm sure it will be rewritten in a few years to include them, but right now I can still pass a house with it. Also, I inspect the house; yards aren't really my focus. If a part of the yard doesn't affect the house, I don't mess with it."

"But this affects the house!" I countered.

"Maybe it does, maybe it doesn't," he said with a shrug. "Interdimensional portals are tricky things. Has it done anything yet?"

"Well, no, not yet. But it might do something, right? I'm just concerned that it's here and I don't know what it does. What do they do?"

"Oh, lots of things... or nothing. It's hard to say."

"That's neither helpful nor acceptable," I said.

"Maybe you can get away with ignoring it," he said.

"I don't even know if I can ignore it because I don't evenaqqqqqq really know what they do. What are the risks? Can I even touch the damn thing?"

"An interdimensional portal is a gate to either another dimension or just another location in spacetime, like a doorway or a tunnel. It could really go anywhere and you might not want to be there. So I wouldn't go touching it if I were you. Of course, what you do is your own business. I ain't touching it at least." He scratched the back of his head, near the ear where he had stored his pen. "I'm no portal expert, but I've seen a few in my time. They can expel some trash, some funny smells, and maybe some noise. Only rarely does something dangerous come out of it. You got kids or pets?"

"We have a cat, but she's an indoor cat," I said.

"That's good. You don't want her wandering into the portal. You can lose things in it. Then it would be time for a new cat."

"But how do I get rid of it? Because I don't like what I'm hearing. Maybe it isn't a problem today, but it still doesn't sound like something I want on my property." I thought again of his idea that something dangerous might come out of it. And there were even bigger practical reasons. "I'm also concerned that it's probably going to kill the property value when we go to sell."

"Yup," he said, "definitely a deal killer. Occasionally there are some folks who actually want one - y'know, like the people who want to buy a haunted house. Not many, though. You'd probably want to conceal it with bushes."

I looked down to my recently cut bushes. "I think I already fell victim to that. But if they update the housing code like you think, I may not have that option."

He nodded. "So I guess getting rid of it does makes sense, but that's dicey. No good way to go about it. There are really two ways I've seen or heard of people dealing with it. The first involves calling a specialist."

"Yeah," I said. "A specialist sounds what I'm looking for. Do they have a title? Where can I find them?"

"So a specialist doesn't mean a portal specialist really," he said, his voice changing as he began to hedge about the subject. "Just someone who specializes in this thing. The weird stuff. Usually priests, exorcists, magicians, psychics, that sort of thing. All frauds, if you ask me. I've never really heard of one going well, and some don't do anything other than lighten your wallet. I say you look around on your own if you think you're going to do that. Can't recommend it, though."

"So there's a second way?" I asked.

"Yup. So there's a prevailing theory on why portals show up in someone's home. That theory says that the reason why the portal has popped up is something stuck in it, like an item or a lost child. Often something strange, like a crystal skull or some book. Weird stuff. But if that is brought back to this side of the portal, it usually closes up pretty quickly. Just get the item out. That's what I hear, at least. Haven't seen it myself."

"But isn't that basically the same as those specialists?" I said. "It still sounds like I'd be calling someone to get whatever is causing the blockage out."

"Many of those specialists ain't going to actually do something," he said. "And it's been sort of proven - not by me, mind you - that if you get the missing item out, the portal goes away. That's like science or something."

"Are you proposing that I go through the portal?" I said, shocked.

"No, of course not," he said, his voice more reassuring. "You just need someone to go through it for you. Adventurers. Heroes. They love this sort of thing. I suggest you find yourself a hero."

3

As much as it would be convenient, I found that heroes were not listed in the yellow pages and every reference on the internet about heroes was either related to works of fiction or roleplaying games. While I had seen various heroic private investigators on television, I had no luck in finding one on my own. I eventually had to place an ad of my own.

I thought that it would have been a waste of time, as my wife thought, and I would not receive a single serious response. I'm not sure why I finally even decided to post the ad. I think I was tired of seeing the shimmering portal in the backyard. Regardless of my reasons or hopes, I placed the ad and waited.

I received three responses.

I explained to each what I required from them: to dive into the portal, find whatever was keeping it open, and deal with it. I also explained that under no circumstances was I paying any money up front. They either solve my problem, or they don't get paid. Despite these terms, all three were interested.

The first was a young man who couldn't possibly be older than twenty-one. He carried his own sword, which he cradled lovingly. He wore an old deerstalker hat which made him look even more awkward. He sheepishly told me that he had only done this once before, but it had worked out well. I didn't press for details, but he said that after that experience he was now ready for life as an adventurer. Far be it from me to judge, I led him out to the back yard to see the portal. He took a look at the shimmer gate and shivered. I asked him if he was sure he wanted to go. He paused for a moment, his face revealing a clash of emotions, but he nodded anyway. I watched him take a deep breath and jump into the portal.

It was a strange experience watching him go. He was there and then he wasn't, as if he was obscured by a wall I could not see. The portal itself was unchanged, just a shimmering disc standing on its own. I worried about him. Though he called himself a hero, ultimately he was a kid with a sword and I had no idea what was on the other side. Out of that almost fatherly concern, I decided to wait for him. I stood in my yard in front of the portal for a full hour in worry. When he did not emerge so quickly, it broke some of the tension. I went into the house for some coffee, and when I returned to the portal I pulled up some lawn furniture. And waited.

Three hours later, the sky darkening with dusk, something erupted from the portal. As if thrown up by some gigantic beast, it was ejected and fell to the ground. It came to rest in front of the portal as a warning or a trophy.

It was a deerstalker hat.

The kid never followed.

The second person who had replied to my ad was more of what I expected of a hero. He was young but not too young, robust, and good looking. He had short, blond, blow-dried hair and wore impossibly black wraparound sunglasses. He wore a black leather jacket with an obvious bulge for a shoulder-holstered gun. His manner reflected his appearance: slick, calm, and in control. After the inexperience with the kid, I welcomed his professional attitude and can-do charm. We exchanged brief introductions, and then I led him back to the portal, which he entered without fear. Then I stood alone by the portal, feeling good about the experience. I didn't wait outside as I had done with the kid. I went inside my home and went about my business, confident that in a short while I'd hear a knock at the back door, my problem solved.

Six hours later, I was worried. Of course I had my doubts at the three hour mark and a lingering suspicion at the five hour mark, but it was outright worry at six hours. That's when I went out back, carrying a flashlight. I had hoped that I'd find the hero wiping dirt off his leather jacket, a triumphant expression on his face. I didn't find him at all. I only found his sunglasses laying in the dirt in front of the portal.

The third person that applied to my ad was something else entirely. Even if I hadn't had the unfortunate experiences of the first two, I would have been disappointed with this third. His exact age was difficult to guess, but without a doubt, he was old, incredibly old. He had crazy white hair and wrinkles. Yes, exactly the picture you just had in your mind. He did have a charming smile due to dentures, but I just didn't have any confidence in him being heroic or solving my problem. He cited the brown bomber jacket he wore, which displayed a WWII fighter plane on fire and the title "The Blazing 51st!" I tried to talk him out of going into the portal, noting that it was already late in the evening, but he just wouldn't take no for an answer. I led him to the portal reluctantly and hoped the otherworldliness would dissuade him or make him realize this wasn't what he thought. But he was not surprised by the portal. He looked at it and nodded in acknowledgement. He turned to smile at me. Then with a shout of "Tally-ho!" he jumped into that shimmering gate.

I didn't bother waiting up for him, my confidence in him so low. I made myself a stiff drink and questioned my actions. I had let him go into the portal. Surely that made me responsible if he got hurt, right? He was just an old man. In my guilt, I drank myself into numbness and climbed into bed next to my wife who had retired to sleep without even telling me goodnight. The next morning when I woke, I returned to the portal. A pair of dentures awaited me.

I remember sitting at my desk with my head in my hands, staring at the hat, sunglasses, and dentures, wondering what I should do. Should I bury the items? Should I look for relatives? Should I alert the police? After a long time spent staring, I still didn't have a good answer. I put all three items in an old shoebox, then put the shoebox in the far back of a closet, hoping I never stumbled upon the shoebox again.

4

For a while, I tried ignoring the portal. This worked for a time, but the portal was still there in the backyard, always shimmering. I would be having my morning coffee and I'd happen to glance out the back window to see the mysterious gate still in my yard, mocking me. And my wife. I'm pretty sure it was mocking my wife too, though she didn't see it that way. She didn't understand.

I tried hiding the portal, so at least we would not see it. I planted new shrubbery in front of it and behind it. This would also prevent any stray cats or raccoons from easily wandering into it. In front of the shrubs I planted flowers, trying to turn an ugly problem into a beautiful yard feature. This actually worked, but only for a time. But during that period, there was peace. My morning coffee was uninterrupted, our household was unmocked.

But like in all things, hiding a problem is not a permanent situation. The peace did not last. If the portal could not be seen, it would make its effects apparent. The plants and flowers around the portal began to... change. Maybe mutate would be a better word. I don't know if something spilled out of the portal onto them, or if it was simply the interdimensional equivalent of latent radiation, but all vegetation in proximity changed. Most twisted and sprouted, erupting in a rainbow of colored flowers and stalks. These were strange, but they had their own beauty. The rainbow of colors was the pleasant part. The other plant mutations were far less tolerable.

A few of the flowers took to singing. Not just occasionally, but near constantly. They were loud enough to be heard in my office and my bedroom, though thankfully not most of the house. You may think this would have been a boon, something to work with in my favor, but it was not. You might think this could have been my million dollar act that I could take on whatever passes for vaudeville these days – daytime talk shows, late night celebrity cattle calls, I guess. But no, the problem was their voices. They didn't sing well. While there was an initial novelty, no one would want to listen to this. They sung painful off-key renditions of once-popular songs, like *Copa Cabana*, *Mandy*, or *The Macarena*. It was like having a karaoke bar permanently installed in my backyard. I found myself awake late at night, being unable to sleep through a flower's extended version of *Total Eclipse of the Heart*. I envied my wife's prescription sleep medicine she had for a preexisting problem. She slept like a log through every encore of *Uptown Girl*.

The singing wore on my mind and my body as they kept me from getting a good night's sleep. After a week of this horrible serenade, lying awake in bed for hours at a time, I had enough - it was time for what passed as violence in my life. In the garage I found myself a pair of yard clippers and a flashlight. Minutes later I entered the backyard as a murderer of flowers. With extreme prejudice, I cut the stem of the flower currently singing. The flower let out an "Urk!" sound and fell to the ground. For a moment, there was silence and my manic grin grew wider. Then what happened next shattered all my hopes and made me want to cry.

The severed flower began screaming.

A loud shrill scream erupted from the flower's mouth. When it ran out of "breath", it paused for a moment and then let out a new scream. I tried stamping the flower with my foot, but that just made it scream louder. The screaming was much louder than the singing and I knew my neighbors could hear it. I felt like I had just set off a house alarm that I couldn't shut off. I shook the severed flower, trying to get it to shut up. I went inside and grabbed a throw pillow from the couch and tried to smother the flower. All that did was muffle the sound, but the screaming continued. At a loss, I grabbed duct tape and tried taping the flower back on. After holding the severed flower to the stem for a few seconds, lining it up so that I could tape it, a funny thing happened. The stem reattached itself, healing the break. One second there was a gap, and then a second later there wasn't. I quickly pulled back my hand. I expected the flower to look at me reproachfully and ask for some sort of apology, but there was no such reaction. Instead there was a moment of pause, after which the flower dramatically cleared its throat. Then it began singing. Now it sang opera.

I guess that was sort of an improvement.

5

I finally broke down and decided to pursue the other route: specialists. I knew that the inspector had warned me against them, but singing and screaming flowers were far beyond my limit of sanity and my marriage. My wife was deciding to spend more and more time away from the house and I was sure it was the flowers. Flowers of singing evil.

Since I was not the most devout of worshippers and had not been to any church service in over a decade, I didn't have a trusted priest, preacher, or deacon to call upon. I contacted the local church and after much groveling and the promise of a large donation, the priest came out. He came out in casual plainclothes, and if not for the Roman collar, I would not have realized he was ordained.

I showed him the offending flowers and the portal. Of course he was shocked, but once he overcame that, he didn't have the best of news for me. He admitted that while he agreed that the portal and particularly the flowers were an abomination and affront against God, a point driven home by the flowers singing *Ave Maria* behind him, he had never seen this sort of thing before and he had no idea how he could actually help. I suggested an exorcism, but he shook his head. It turned out the Catholic church had very strict circumstances under which that was done and the priest expected this request would be turned down. He said that he'd check, since he had personally witnessed the abominable flowers, but not to hold my breath. He patted me on the shoulder for reassurance, since that was the only thing he could do for me.

The next candidate in the endless cavalcade of failure was a voodoo guy. He corrected me that he was in fact a Vodoun Houngan. The difference was of no particular note to me, but I conceded if he was able to help me, I would call him whatever he liked and gain a new appreciation for his faith. When he saw the yard, he nodded stoically, taking a keen eye to examine the flowers that were now in an off-pitch choral rendition of *You Are My Sunshine*. He took some time to peer through the bushes at the portal.

"Papa Legba be none too happy 'bout portal," he said, using an accent I was sure was fake. "He consider it a personal insult."

"That's great!" I said. "So we can get rid of it!"

The man shook his head. "As much as he don't be likin' it, dis ain't Papa Legba's problem. Dis be your own path tah walk. Papa Legba would give you his blessin' tah walk it, a bit of his power followin' witcha. But you go dis way alone."

Path to walk? Did he mean through the portal? Of course I wasn't climbing into the portal. That was a ridiculous idea.

"So no, you can't help me," I said.

He shook his head. "You know where dis needs tah go. Dere ain't none who will do it for yah."

"It's money, isn't it?" I said. "You want more money." I hadn't paid him anything yet, so anything more than zero would be more.

He shook his head more vigorously. "Don't be insultin' dah loa." He packed up his bag of weird tools. "If a fool yah be, you be it alone." He left.

6

I awoke in the middle of the night to some noise in the back. I went to the window and looked down into the yard. In the moonlight I saw a figure standing near the portal's location. He was using what appeared to be a battleaxe to chop down the shrubs I had used to conceal the portal.

Looking him over, I knew what he was. He was big and buff, like a weight lifter about to roid rage. But he had flowy blonde hair that made me think he was a Viking come down from Valhalla. He was shirtless, a belt with many pouches holding up his leather pants. He was someone out of a movie or comic book and definitely not someone who should be doing unauthorized gardening in my yard in the middle of the night. But I still knew what he was. He was another hero.

I realized now that heroes would come even if I didn't put out an ad. There was something essential in the interdimensional portal that just called them. Heroes would come, seeking to right the wrong that caused this rip in space, or at very least to find the adventure through the portal which they would never find in our world. The portal was a magnet for them and I realized I could not stop them.

Then I wondered if it was a greater problem than I had realized at first. What if they had been coming this entire time? I hadn't been looking for signs of their passage, so maybe I had missed footprints and lost items. They could have been making attempts on the portal and failing this whole time. How many had been lost in the portal while seeking adventure? And what did they find there?

When this hero had finished clearing the shrubs from portal, he looked around guiltily. I saw him look at the house, but I don't think he saw me at the darkened window. In the moonlight I saw his face and read all the emotions there - the trepidation, the anxious excitement, the nerves steeled against danger. Then he hefted his axe and leapt into the portal.

When morning came, I investigated the yard. I found his axe laying in the mud by the decapitated shrubs. It was chipped and stained with blood.

7

Was the portal alive? Had the inspector been wrong? Was it not a gate through space and time? Maybe it was only a mouth, a hungry maw which devoured all that stepped through it. It was a cursed thing, and its misfortune was not contained by it. Its unholy energy stretched out to destroy all that was around it. Now it had begun affecting my marriage.

Oh, she claimed that the portal itself wasn't a big deal. She admitted it was weird, but that wasn't her issue. My wife said the problem was that I was obsessed with the portal. She said that since I had discovered it, I had done nothing but worry about it. She pointed to the journal and spreadsheets I kept on it. She noted how many hours I spent researching and looking for help. She even reminded me of the shrine-like area where I kept the items left behind by those adventurers; in my research I had decided to take the shoebox out of the closet and keep the objects where I could look at them in case I had an idea. I also wanted to save the items on the unlikely chance the heroes returned to reclaim them. My wife was particularly disturbed by the bloody battleaxe. That might have been what started the discussion.

She said that my worry, my frenetic obsession with the portal in the yard, was stressing her out. Her other concern was all that time spent on the portal was spent away from the marriage. She claims I was absent from the relationship. In a certain turn of phrase, she suggested I was engaging in infidelity with the time-space anomaly in the back yard.

It was clear that she didn't understand the gravity of the situation we lived under. There was an ill shadow cast by the portal, one that fell upon our entire household. We weren't safe. Reality was warping around that gate, strange heroes were traipsing through our yard with lethal weapons at their leisure, and who knows what might come out of the portal? Who knew what was on the other side of it? I sure didn't, but at times I wondered...

In any event, I was sure she really didn't understand how important this was. I had tried to explain it to her many times before, but she has never really gotten it. Rather than try to explain again, I decided I'd try to address her concerns. At length I assured her that I loved her and I was part of this marriage, not an absentee by any stretch, but I needed to solve this problem for the safety of our house and family. When it was once and for all solved, then I could rest, returning my energy back to her and our marriage. And then things would be good again. But until then, the portal was a serious danger and I needed to devote *all* my spare time to it.

I said this all with a calmness and a smile so that she would know I wasn't being antagonistic or treating her like she was dumb or didn't understand. It was for the best of us. So I went through it all, slowly and carefully, making sure she got the right impression and she knew where I stood.

This was the wrong answer.

8

What followed were a number of days of hot arguments and cold shoulders. It was a volatile situation and I knew not whether it would change from hot to cold until I opened my mouth. Naturally, I tried to lay low in my office as often as possible, my only companion the cat who for some reason loved sleeping on the printer.

It was during this time that I came across the website of Trans Dimensional Anomaly Solutions. It was a slick website talking about the various services they offered. They had a description of a portal, though it was dressed up in corporate talk, I guess maybe to be easier to sell to venture capital investors. But it was still obvious that meant portals. I worried that they did not service my area, since they were located in San Jose, California, but I saw that they worked with contractors across the country. I filled out their contact form so I could get a call back to discuss how they can help me.

I received a call two hours later. On the phone, Vickie, their Solutions Concierge, reviewed the information I had sent them. She had a very professional manner and I felt hopeful that they would be able to help me. When I flat out said the word "Portal", she did not pause nor change her demeanor. It was soon certain: they helped with portals. And they were willing to help me.

There was a fee - of course there was a fee. But it was a reasonable enough fee if they could do what none could do. Then they set a time - between eight and noon on Tuesday morning. I wasn't a fan of the open ended appointment, feeling like they were installing cable rather than helping with an entrance to dimensions unknown, but I was willing to overlook that.

Tuesday didn't come quick enough and I found myself up early, dressed, and sipping coffee as eight AM came around. I didn't expect them there right at eight, but I was ready. They finally showed up at half past twelve. I was on hold waiting for a Concierge at Trans Dimensional Anomaly Solutions when they rang the doorbell. I hung up the phone and answered the door.

They were not what I expected. For all the glitz of the company's website and the professionalism of their support staff over the phone, the men who came out were a disappointment. They showed up in a white van that was in need of a wash. I noticed no logo painted on the van, but then I recalled that the company said they worked with contractors across the country. With dismay, I realized these were the contractors.

There were two of them. They each wore gray coveralls making me think they were car mechanics rather than portal technicians. Their hair was unwashed, their faces unshaven, and they had a very lazy and unprofessional manner.

"You the dude with the portal?" said one.

"Yeah, you're from -"

"TDAS? Yeah, we work for them. But we do other stuff if you need things done. You want free cable? We can do free cable. If your neighbor has wifi, we can probably get you some free internet too. Most people have lame passwords. If your wifi password is your pet's name, you should change it."

"No, I don't need cable or internet," I said tersely, making a mental note to change the router password. "I just want to get the portal fixed. Can you do that?"

"Oh yeah, we can do that, no problem," said the man, turning to bark at the other one. "Jenk, get the machine setup. We got a portal job."

"No cable?" said the other man.

"No, just the portal."

In a short while they had reparked their van in the driveway near the gate to the back yard. The sliding door was opened and a collection of tubes and wires almost fell out, as if they were the van's innards. The two contractors seemed not to be fans of me watching over their every move, so I returned to the house and glanced out the windows occasionally to try to see what was going on. They had a long silver accordion tube, maybe the thickness of a basketball, that stretched from the inside of their van all the way to the portal. I missed the moment when they pushed the tube into the portal, but it seemed unaffected by the gateway and stayed put. Sometime after that I heard them start a machine that was unseen in their van.

The sound was overwhelming, sort of like the sound of a lawnmower, but even louder. I had to actually check to make sure they weren't actually mowing my lawn or taking care of the gardening duties along with their portal solution. But no, the only thing happening in my yard was the silver tube. All the sound came from the interior of the van. When one of the men came back into view, I saw that he was wearing headphones.

This went on for an hour. After that, I went down to talk to the men. I wondered loudly how long the noise would go on for. My wife was luckily at work, but the cat had hidden deep in a closet in fear, and I had to admit it was pretty distracting for me as well.

"It'll be done when it gets done," said the man I spoke to before. A cigarette dangled from his lips. The other man had his legs up in the front of the van, also smoking a cigarette and looking through a pornographic magazine.

"What's it doing exactly?" I asked.

"Sciency stuff," he said in way of answer. When my expression didn't change to anything favorable, he said, "You wouldn't understand. Complicated."

I was beginning to lose my faith in their company. "Do *you* know what it does?"

"Oh sure, sure, I know," he said.

"What does it do?" I asked.

"Sciency stuff," he said. "I sat through a seminar on this. The machine knows what it's doing. It's a smart little machine."

"So you don't know what it does, you just use it," I said with a sigh. "For how long?"

"Until it's done," he said. "I'm not a fan of that either. I get paid for the job, not the hour. I want it done quicker too. But there's really nothing to do until then."

I turned to look at the yard, where there was a now plume of smoke rising.

"Is it supposed to be smoking like that?" I said nervously.

The man turned and looked at the yard. His eyes widened. He ran to the van and slammed his hand down on the hood to get the other's attention. "Smoker! Smoker!"

The other man threw down his magazine and leapt into action. Carrying a full sized fire extinguisher, he charged through the fence gate to the back yard. A little more slowly followed myself and the first man.

The backyard was on fire. A gout of flame erupted continuously from the portal, melting the tube. All the bushes around the portal were now on fire. The ground in front of the portal looked like it was a blasted ruin. Thankfully, the fire was not near the house and there were no trees or bushes that might lead it there.

The man with the extinguisher had come to a stop, his cigarette dangling from his lips, unsure of what to do with the fire extinguisher.

"Oh Christ," said the man with me. "Jenk, the extinguisher now!"

"What do I spray?" said Jenk.

"*Everything*," said the other man.

I'd like to give Jenk the benefit of the doubt, saying that he fought the good fight, valiantly trying to put out the conflagration in front of me. But that didn't happen. He let loose with the fire extinguisher, spraying that stuff at the base of the flames where it simply sizzled, but it wasn't enough. He moved closer, and that's when his arm lit on fire. He immediately dropped the extinguisher and ran for it. As he ran past us, the flame had begun climbing up his arms.

"Stop, drop and roll, Jenk! Stop, drop, and roll!" called the man next to me. When it appeared that Jenk wasn't doing that, the other man ran to the front of the house after him.

I stayed in the back, watching the flames. I was pretty sure the fire was not going to jump to my house, but I figured I should be sure. In case nobody else had already, I pulled my phone out of my pocket and called 911. I explained the fire, leaving out anything about a portal. They asked the name of the technicians I had out to do the work, so I returned to the front of the house. I walked through the fence gate just in time to hear the screech of tires as the van took off. The silver accordion tube was left on the ground.

"Uh, they just took off," I said with an annoyed sigh. "So I don't know who they are exactly."

The fire department was suspicious when they showed up, but they put out the fire just the same. Their safety inspector berated me on the topic of various possible causes of the fire, then he left with the rest of his crew. Since the backyard had been reduced to a blackened, smoking mess, nobody noticed the shimmering portal. But once they were gone and the smoke abated, the portal was still there.

I'm pretty sure it was mocking me.

9

I'm not sure I can point to an exact moment my marriage started going bad. Yeah, the portal had caused some friction, but was it all truly just the portal? Was it only my mounting obsession? Or had the cracks in the relationship been there before we moved in, an unseen weakness just waiting for a stressor? I will never know. But I can definitely point to the moment when it ended. After the fire, my wife walked out. There had been an argument that night. A very large argument that involved a few kitchen implements thrown with what I hoped was not lethal intent and ending with me sleeping on the couch.

The next day I returned home from work to find her gone. Her clothes gone, her valuables gone, and a long Dear John email in my inbox that read more like a Screw You John email. She even took the cat.

I miss that cat.

TDAS never responded to any of my calls. Neither did my wife. The county offices, however, wanted to talk at length about the damage in my yard. After the first few times of repeating the same story, the official accepting it, and then them calling me back for the "real" story, I stopped responding.

I lost my job. I had taken so much time off of work to research the portal and deal with the TDAS contractors that when it came to the heartache from my wife walking out... well, those days I called in sick were the straw that broke the camel's back. Fired.

I walked the house like I haunted it. It was an empty house full of her absence and methodical research about portals. Knowing that portals technically corresponded to the Threshold phase of Joseph Campbell's Hero's Journey felt worthless now that my life had fallen apart, everything I cared about gone. The backyard might have looked like a blasted wasteland after the fire but the inside of the house felt like one in the wake of all that had happened.

It was an understatement admitting it now: I had messed up. Obsession on protecting my family had caused me to lose them. She wouldn't even return my emails. Every forgotten cat toy I discovered under the furniture made my heart hurt. My life might have well been in that yard when it went up in flames.

Maybe it was just the depression thinking, but in a way, I finally understood the heroes who had been jumping through my portal. When you had nothing - or if your life was so horrible and painful it was worse than nothing - even jumping recklessly into an unknown portal in search of just the slim chance of an adventure appeared better than pulling yourself out of bed every morning to try to find a way up out of the dark hole you lived every day in.

It was a dark realization, the worst kind of clarity. It's the kind of inspiration of bad sense that comes before an even worse decision. It's when you come up with the most terrible choice because it felt so right in your entirely broken life.

It made sense. That was the problem. It made sense for that first moment, and it kept making sense for too long. It made sense when I strapped on some old work boots I hadn't worn in years. It made sense when I packed a backpack full of supplies. It made sense when I pulled on that deerstalker hat, when I put on those sunglasses, when I put those dentures in my pocket for good luck. It made sense when I stood in front of the portal, my fingers nervously tensing and relaxing on the grip of the chipped battleaxe.

I only really questioned it when I was in the midst of leaping through the portal, but at that point it was too late.

I guess I was one of those heroes now.

Zombie Crunch
A Nowak Brothers Story

Gas masks on.

Weapons secured.

Lights fastened.

I grabbed the rope and nodded to my brother Mikkel. Then I dropped down into the darkness of drainage tunnels. I landed fine, my boots twisting on the gritty ground. It was damp from the recent rains. There probably was an odor, but I wasn't getting it through the filter of my mask.

I clicked on my flashlight and pulled out my weapon of choice, a lead pipe, as my brother came down the rope behind me. I shined the light both ways in the tunnel, seeing no danger. I put my pipe back in its holster in my jacket and relaxed.

"What have we got, Szandor?" asked my brother. He wore his mask around his neck, not expecting hazardous air in a drainage tunnel. I was just being careful.

"We're clear," I said, pulling off my mask. "Tunnel is mostly intact."

Mikkel nodded as he glanced around. "Let's get a move on. It's about two blocks above, but who knows how far it is down here."

There were some branches and twists to the tunnel as it connected to drainage rooms, but nothing notable. In twenty minutes we had reached our destination. This was a large cistern-like drainage room. Many pipes fed into it, as well as large passages for maintenance workers and collected water from other chambers. There was a large tunnel that probably led out to the river. From what we could see, there weren't more than puddles at the bottom. At our level ten feet above the rest of the chamber, there was a narrow ledge that circled the room, allowing maintenance workers to check the drains. The room was lit by meager light streaming in through a few grates in the ceiling.

Mikkel shined his flashlight over one of the grates. "That looks to be our drain."

My own light trailed down from it. "And there's our problem."

Some of the cistern's wall had crumbled. A pile of debris stretched from the drain we were interested in to the bottom of the chamber. It didn't look like the structure was damaged, but it had brought down other parts of the room. A large riveted panel had fallen down to cover a side passage. There was a lot of broken masonry, twisted metal, and strangely, a shovel.

We're not itinerant maintenance workers nor are we architects, so the actual damage to the chamber wasn't what we were here for. We're monster hunters, so we were more interested in the creatures that were on that pile of debris.

Zombies.

One was at the top of the pile poking at the grate in question. Another was fumbling around halfway up the pile. I was reminded of roaches crawling on the walls. Below us, I counted five more zombies. Their lumbering gait and dirty clothes tipped me off to the fact that they were old zombies: decaying and slow. Less lethal, but still dangerous for the unprepared.

"This should be easy," I said, pulling out my lead pipe and pulling my mask down.

"Hold on, Szandor, let's check -" started my brother.

I didn't hear the rest of what he said, because I was already jumping down from the ledge, using my momentum to bash a zombie's head in with my lead pipe.

* * *

We were doing this job for the kids.

There aren't a lot of children in our line of work as monster hunters. One ray of light in all this darkness is that kids are usually not the ones in danger in the vast majority of our jobs. But every so often a monster gets where it shouldn't be.

In this case it was a playground.

Someone got hurt so we got the call. Maybelle, owner and motherly bartender at our neighborhood pub, *Twin Eagles*, phoned Mikkel for us to come by. I had never had a bar call me and ask for my presence, so I would have been excited if I didn't suspect that it involved monster hunting. That's generally what happens in our old neighborhood of South Egan where they know what we do.

Once we arrived, Maybelle waved us over. "I knew you two would want to check this out when I heard about it."

She discreetly lead us to the back room reserved for private parties, weddings (fun fact, there has been one wedding in the entire history of Twin Eagles), or just when Maybelle has gotten sick of our shit and needs a break. There was nothing fun going on, but I did spy a woman and her daughter near the billiards table that had never had any balls or cues.

"This is Shelly," said Maybelle in a grave voice. "Her daughter was *bitten*."

"Shit," I breathed. I took a look at Shelly. Thirties, dark hair, dark skin, distraught but trying to stay determined. She was vaguely familiar; I might have seen her around the neighborhood. She had a decade on us, so we wouldn't have run in the same circles.

Mikkel was more social than me. In the time I had stood there sizing them up he had already introduced himself to the mother and now squatted at eye level in front of the little girl. "Hi, I'm Mikkel."

"Hi," was all the girl said in response, but it was success getting that much out of her. She must have been six years old and her eyes were puffy with tears. She wore a yellow raincoat, her formerly braided hair now a mess.

"Can I see the bite?" asked Mikkel gently.

The girl paled and hid her face in her mother's coat. Mikkel looked up at Shelly with kind eyes, letting his expression do the asking. The mother looked down at her daughter. "Charlie, can I show the young man your ouchie?"

The girl looked up at her mother for a long moment, then finally gave a slow nod. She slowly held out her right hand - not to Mikkel, but to her mom. Her mom delicately peeled back a bandage, the girl wincing but bravely keeping her arm out.

Mikkel took a look at the wound and nodded. I arched my neck to see without stepping forward. A familiar wound. Bite pattern, whitish coloring where the teeth went deep.

"How long has it been?" I asked.

The girl was suddenly scared of me and Shelly threw me a dirty look. Mikkel looked at the girl and gently said, "Thank you for your help." The girl smiled weakly and her mother reapplied the bandage.

"Earlier today," answered Maybelle. "Five hours, maybe."

I let out a sigh of relief. Still in the early period and very treatable.

Mikkel stood up and addressed Shelly. "Take her to a clinic."

"We tried to go to a pediatrician, but without insurance we can't get in before next week," said Shelly nervously.

Mikkel shook his head. "That's too late and they don't know what to do. Go to the clinic over on Blesden. You'll probably get Vitaly, but either way, tell them she was playing around rotten wood and she jabbed herself with it."

"That looks nothing like -" started Shelly.

Mikkel calmly stopped her with a hand held up. "Just tell them that. She'll get the medicine she needs and she'll be fine."

"Where did this happen?" I asked.

"Keeler Park, by the playground," said Maybelle.

"The park?" I said incredulously.

This sounded bizarre. As it should, because that girl had been bitten by a zombie.

* * *

The zombie collapsed to the floor dead. My falling attack had killed it in a single blow. I felt real good about that. I steadied myself and hefted my lead pipe for another attack. There were four zombies down here and two above me. The four immediately turned and came at me. One of them was indeed old and clumsy, but the other three were surprisingly fast. They closed on me quickly. I swung at the first and got his shoulder instead of his head. He stumbled a few feet but stayed on his feet. The other two lunged at me.

Behind me there was a *shing!* sound as my brother unsheathed his katana. He had dropped down silently while I made all the noise. He beheaded the zombie that had stumbled.

The two that lunged at me missed with their arms, but their bodies crowded me, their heads trying to find someplace to bite. With a roar I flung my arms up, pushing the zombies off me.

I loved this. The thrill of fighting, winning, being useful. With something almost like glee, I swung at the head of one of the zombies.

* * *

Keeler Park was a sad little park by nearly any definition. It was the only bit of green space in the South Egan area and it was small. It was maybe the size of a single apartment building or suburban house lot. It was poorly maintained in a poor neighborhood. The concrete sidewalks were cracked in many places, the basketball court had been missing their hoops since 1998, and the spinny Merry Go Round hadn't spun since I was seven. That left one slide, a surprisingly functional set of monkey bars, two benches, and exactly three trees.

It wasn't much, but if it was all you had, you made sure to use it.

Due to the sparse nature of the park, it took us about five seconds to confirm there were no zombies. Just puddles and a sense of desolation. I'm sure that after little Charlie was bitten, there was some neighborhood call for everyone to avoid the park.

We had gotten some additional information about the attack. Charlie said there was a man in the ground who wanted to shake hands. And when she tried to shake, he stung her. It sounded like a description of some strange nightmare, but it was what we were working with.

A few minutes of walking around revealed that the basketball court had drainage grates. We knelt down and looked at the them. The slats had about two inches of space between them. Easy for a kid to stick her hand through and get bitten. We shined our flashlight through the grates. That didn't reveal very much. We *thought* we might have seen movement down one of them, but that could have been a shadow, or a rat, or fucking nothing.

We sat down on one of the benches. My butt got wet since I didn't wipe if off first.

"Well, what do we think?" I said.

Mikkel shrugged. "The drains are the only things it could be."

"Kid sticks her hand in grate, gets bitten? How'd the zombie get there? Why is the zombie there?"

"That's what we're here to find out," said Mikkel.

"It's not much to go on."

"Yeah, but we don't want any other kids getting hurt, so I'm willing to go the extra mile."

I admitted he had a point. "Wish we could just open the grates," I complained. The drain was set into the concrete and did not have a hinge nor screws. We'd have to break the concrete to open it from here. While effective, then the city would have to come out and fix it, and I did not trust the city - probably New Avalon Water & Power - to get something in South Egan fixed with any expediency. Neither of us wanted to leave the kids in a park with a broken hole to the drainage tunnels.

"Let's figure out how to get down there," said Mikkel.

"Drainage tunnel at the river?" I suggested.

"We don't know which one and they'd probably be pretty wet right now. I'd rather go in from above. I'd rather look down on zombies than run into them. Above is safer in case there are surprises."

* * *

My lead pipe connected with the zombie's head with a satisfying sound. Blood, brains, and teeth splattered across the room. I let out a whoop of excitement as I turned toward the other zombie. After this one there were just three more and we'd be done.

There was a surprise.

I heard a chorus of growls from the darkness behind me near the tunnel to the river. I turned quickly to see a group of zombies rushing from the shadows. Fast, strong, fresh. I had begun to curse in frustration when the zombie I turned my back on leapt upon me.

* * *

We found an entrance to the drainage tunnels two blocks away after a flurry of phone calls, exchanged favors, and agreeing two purchase two pizzas a delivery driver was stuck with after a prank call. Not far from Keeler Park was *Pedro's Prodigious Pizzas*. No one called it that. Old residents called it *Pedro's* or *peepee* if you had grown up as an annoying kid here. Lately they were trying to rebrand as *P3*. I had no idea if that was working for them.

The guy who greeted us wore a shirt that had the name Pedro, but he introduced himself as Mateo. He told us he could help, especially after he heard what happened to the kid. In the old neighborhood, people generally knew what we did and tended not to think we were full of shit. When they saw the bite marks, they took us more seriously.

In the basement, behind a palette of flat pizza boxes and a rusted pizza oven they had never been able to get rid of, was a trap door. This lead to the drainage tunnels.

"Lucky for you guys, everything is cleared off the hatch," said Mateo.

"Yeah, that does save time," I agreed.

"It's convenient for you that those other guys came through last week," said Mateo.

"Wait, other guys?" asked Mikkel.

"Yeah, they musta come back up somewhere else, because they never came back through here. I kept it unlocked for a couple days just in case."

"Who were they?" I asked.

"Maintenance guys, I think," said Mateo. "Avalon Water and Power."

* * *

I roared in frustration, rolling my shoulders to fling the zombie off my back. That gave me just a moment of free air before one of the new zombies rushed into me. He was a big guy wearing a high visibility vest.

His jumpsuit beneath had the logo for New Avalon Water and Power. His nametag said he had been Steve.

Steve had some weight on me, so his charge hit me and we kept going as I stumbled backward. We slammed into the piece of metal that had fallen to block a tunnel. There was a large clank as we hit and I took the brunt of that impact in the currency of pain. Up close I could see that Steve was missing much of his left shoulder and the left side of his neck where he had been gnawed upon. I guessed that was as far as the other zombies got before he rose as one of the undead. They never ate each other. Zombies devouring each other would be convenient for us. I guess they have some sort of professional courtesy.

Steve tried to lean in to bite me and I held him back in a situation that was probably too familiar in my career. What was interesting to me was the sound of metal straining behind me. And by interesting, I mean it was starting to worry me. I also heard some gurgling.

I pushed forward and the zombie Steve slammed me back into the metal plate again with more pain and a louder clang. My gas mask was dislodged, half off my face. Now the metal straining sound was even louder and I could hear water clearly.

"Mikkel, I think we have a problem!" I shouted, hoping my brother could hear me, though I couldn't see him.

"A little busy here!" responded Mikkel.

"Mikkel, we have a *huge* problem!"

I fought forward, trying to get away from the metal plate and the creaking, straining noises of what it was holding back. I got a few steps forward, but then Steve and another Water and Power zombie slammed me back hard, their jaws snapping at me.

And that's when the dam broke.

It wasn't actually a dam, it was the piece of metal debris which had gotten wedged in front of the drainage tunnel, keeping rainwater from entering this room and draining out to the river. It had been pretty rainy lately, so there was a lot of water waiting behind it.

This wasn't some countdown situation where water rose to our feet and we had a minute to bemoan our fate and try to get out. The metal piece bent, and then suddenly it and I were flung forward, water filling almost the whole room immediately. I remember being shot forward to hit the wall of the cistern. Then I was churned upward for a moment before I was yanked down as the massive wave swirled around the room to the exit. I fought to get my head up above the dirty rapids as I was pulled out the drainage tunnel. I managed to get my face out for a split second, getting one half breath and a lungful of water.

Then I was dragged under, pulled along, and spit out.

* * *

I came to on the riverbank. I saw the abandoned warehouses of the Husks across the river from me and above me was the fence on the edge of South Egan. I was dripping wet and covered with filth. My gas mask had been ripped off me and my lead pipe was gone.

I pulled myself to my feet and looked for danger. There were a couple zombies on the riverbank, but most of them were floating in the river, slowly moving toward the lake. I didn't see any of them move, so I hoped those were already dead.

I shook my head, trying to get my senses back. Down the river bank two dozen paces was Mikkel. I stumbled toward him as he stood over a zombie that was laying on the bank. It struggled like a turtle on its back. Mikkel raised his katana and stabbed the point through the zombie's head. It stopped moving.

"What the hell happened?" said Mikkel as I reached him.

"I told you we had a huge problem," I said, water from my head dripping into my mouth as I spoke. It tasted terrible.

"That's an understatement," he said. "I didn't know it was catastrophic. Usually we have code words for really bad."

"I don't think we have any emergency shorthand for *we're going to drown*," I replied.

Mikkel nodded. Then he looked up at the fences on either side of the riverbank. Two people had already started looking at the bodies floating in the river.

"We need to disappear, like immediately," he said.

"Agreed," I said. "We need to get out of here before we hear sirens."

* * *

We didn't have any trouble with the police. We knew this side of town too well, so we were nowhere to be found when the police finally showed up. From what we heard, they were out there in boats until the wee hours looking for corpses. Maybe they had been even dredging the river.

When all was said and done, the local news didn't mention zombies. The best we could find was a story about mysterious medical waste dumping. I guess either unclaimed corpses fell under "mysterious medical waste" or someone was trying real hard to cover things up.

Authentic Avalon was a little more adventurous. It had a headline about "Katana-Wielding Executioners Stalking the Lower East Side!" Closer to the truth, but it didn't exactly paint us in the best light. No zombies mentioned either.

The kids were safe. It didn't matter if the news didn't report it or anyone knew we had done it. What needed to be done got done. The zombies had been cleared out of that cistern and were unlikely to return. We wanted to check it out to see if the debris had been moved in the deluge, but the police were all over the drainage tunnels looking for a source of the bodies. We needed to avoid those tunnels for a while.

All's well that ends well, right?

I wasn't so sure. I still had sinking feelings about this one. Zombies had just been washed down the river. They all looked dead and no one had reported any cannibal attacks along the edges of the river or lake. But they had only *looked* dead. What if one was alive? What if this just started a whole new infection on the other side of the lake?

The Last Ghost

1

The candlestick holder clattered to the floor and rolled halfway across the room. Again.

My concentration broken, I stood from where I sat working on Mother's estate, hard at work and hoping that once I finished with it I could rejoin my beloved Joanna. Crossing the room, I bent to pick up the candlestick holder again. I still couldn't find the candle itself on the floor. I put the holder back with the other three. Wrought iron and plated with silver, they were part of a set of candlestick holders my family had owned for decades. They matched four in the dining area. These four had originally been in Mother's sitting room. The other three still had candles, it was only this one that was falling over repeatedly.

Under the watchful eye of the ghost, I sat back down at the desk. I knew that he wasn't the one who had been knocking over the candlestick holder. All he did was watch, which was unnerving in its own way. No matter which room of the house I was in, he was there. Whether he was standing still and stately like the grandfather clock he stood next to, whether he loomed over me in the water closet, or if he was half inside the wall and staring out from behind a picture of my aunt, he was there. The place he was might differ, but his presence was always the same. Sometimes I had to look for him, finding him in a dark corner, or half hidden by an Oriental screen my grandfather had brought back from another country, but there was no place in the house I could avoid him. He never appeared to move. Either he just appeared in each room as I entered it, or he was in one place that seemed to look out on every place in the house at once, as if he were the multiplied reflection of a shattered mirror.

I called him the Butler. This was due to his ubiquitous nature, his shabby old fashioned suit, and the look on his face. He had the mask of controlled facial features I so commonly associate with servants. Impassive so as not to offend, their faces kept placid so that their masters could easily confuse them with the furniture if necessary. But the Butler's face was marred. Not with blood or ash, as you might expect from a ghost. No, his face was marred with *emotion*. Not much, but just enough that I noticed. Behind his impassive face, there was something breaking through. It was not fully shown on his face, as if the moment of death had stopped it from fully emerging and etching itself across his face like some strange butterfly coming out of chrysalis. But if you looked closely, if you knew what you were looking for, if you were used to dealing with household servants, you might just notice it.

It was revulsion.

Maybe there was a little shock mixed in, but it was essentially one emotion. The Butler's ghostly face was stuck in a fixed mask of ill-concealed revulsion. It was this face that I saw at every hour, either standing in plain sight or vaguely hidden as I walked through the empty house and worked on the estate. I came to think that he was silently judging me, that his revulsion was meant for me, but I had no proof he even knew me other than the fact that he stared at me.

Though the Butler's presence was unsettling, he was relatively benign. He just stared and watched. While that alone put my nerves on end, more so since I was alone in the house, it did not have as great a reaction as you might expect. There was something very familiar in the Butler's presence. It occurred to me that the Butler may not have been new. The new aspect may be just that I now *noticed* him. I supposed that in all the years I spent in this house, the one I grew up in, that he may have been ever present but just out of my ability to perceive. I had always been a somewhat oblivious child, so that I realized my own failing now in adulthood would not be so surprising. I knew not whether to be comforted or further unsettled by the probable fact of the Butler's constant and time honored existence.

I only wished that he'd stop staring. If he thought me encroaching on his territory - even if it had been my family's home for generations - then he had to just simply wait until I had Mother's estate in order before I would leave the house forever.

I'd like to say that he was the only problem I encountered. I'd like to say that he was the only ghost, even the last ghost, but he was just the first.

2

The second ghost was the Madam. I encountered her when I nearly walked through her. I had been leaving the study, taking a break from the estate work. I almost lost my balance recoiling from the pale woman that was standing right in front of me. She did not move but instead seemed frozen in her position. Her right arm was out straight, pointing at something unseen. Her left hand was held at her mouth, as if to cover her face in shock and disgust. Her skin was white, as if powdered with chalk, her makeup still recognizable under the heavy covering.

I called her the Madam because of her age and dress. She was perhaps a few years older than me. Her dress seemed quite matronly to me, giving me the idea of a mother or a well-cared-for wife. The wedding band on her left hand, ever held near her face, confirmed that idea.

My initial shock and unease at her appearance gave way to confusion. I first thought she was accusing. Then I thought she was trying to tell me something. But I came to suspect that her emotional reaction, frozen on her face and form, was merely coincidental to her current location. Like the Butler, I found the Madam in a variety of places in the house. While I had found her pointing at me a number of times, so too had I found her pointing at a variety of other things, for example, at the grandfather clock near the stairwell, at the candlestick holder that had rolled across the floor, and at one of the many framed family pictures which covered the walls.

Unlike the Butler, she did not stay in one place in each room. Sometimes as I walked through a room, I might find her reappearing just to my left or beyond a door. I never saw her move; if I fixed my eyes upon her, her form and the object of her accusations would never waver. No, she would only shift when my eyes were elsewhere. While I still felt shock of seeing a pale woman where I expected none or simply the flare of fear of something different in the corner of my eyes, like the Butler she also appeared benign.

I kept returning to the idea was that she was trying to tell me something, that her extended finger would indicate something of importance either to her or myself. When taking a break from my work on the estate, I did try to line up the Madam's digit with anything which might be important. As I mentioned, she did appear to focus on our grandfather clock, but outside of when it needed to be wound, that did not seem to be of note. She also did seem to point at the door to Mother's sitting room, but since I had closed that room and avoided it, I did not consider this an important lead to follow. In fact, there was only one particular incident after her arrival and before the emergence of the other ghosts that I thought significant.

I found her pointing in the hall at a portrait. I remember at the time being curious about this behavior, as in this case she did not point from across the room. The distance from her finger to the portrait was little more than a foot, leaving no doubt as to what she was trying to indicate. I remember walking up to her, seeing the Butler standing behind her and continuing to silently judge me, as I moved closer to the portrait. This was a photograph, not a painting. It showed my mother, but not as a young girl, but older, in the winter of her middle age, as I had known her most during my life. But as I narrowed my eyes, trying to determine the significance, I came to notice what I believe the Madam wanted me to see. Someone had written something in the dust that lay on the glass in front of the portrait. It said in cursive: *I'm sorry.*

I didn't recognize the hand - no, the finger-writing. There was something familiar in how the letter *I* was shaped and the curve of the *Rs*, but being neither a handwriting expert nor someone who spent much time mastering his own cursive, I was unfamiliar with the identity of the mysterious writer. It occurred to me that it could have been the Madam herself, but I knew not how her unmoving form could write it nor what she would want to apologize to me about.

I remember that I lifted the portrait frame off the wall, wondering if anything could be found on the back. I found the most curious part was not on the portrait or frame. From the frame's hook dripped a single drop of blood. I checked my hands for a wound but found none. Turning back to the drop, I noticed that it slowly trickled down the wall, as if it were some sort of falling tear.

I admit that my reaction was not exactly sensible for what I was witnessing. I count myself glad that I did not scream, but neither did I attempt to explore the strange phenomenon. Instead, I quickly and numbly put the frame back on the hook and left the hall more hastily than I like to admit. When I returned later and in more presence of mind to investigate, I found no trace of the blood.

Whatever the Madam was trying to say was lost on me. It was for the later ghosts to try to tell me.

3

The third ghost didn't show me anything. But he did disturb me far more than the Butler or the Madam.

Whereas the Butler stood staring and the Madam was frozen midpoint, the Child moved. He even spoke.

"Tick tock, tick tock!" came a voice. I dropped my pen immediately, my entire body tensed at the sound in the house which should be empty. Then followed the laughter of a child.

While the Butler was ever present and the Madam would find me if she wanted to be seen, the Child seemed to want me to play a game of hide and seek. I crept through the house, looking for the source of the sound. During this time, I continued to hear the boy say "Tick tock, tick tock!" His giggling would inevitably follow. I knew that he was commenting on the ever present sound of the grandfather clock which could be heard from any room in the house. But the clock was normal and it was the Child's words which invaded my empty house, so he claimed all my attention.

The Madam appeared to be trying to help as I found her pointing at the locked door to Mother's sitting room. This room was of course off-limits, so I ignored the Madam's suggestion. Should all other searching fail and the Child was in that room, I might break the taboo, but this was not the time. Any doubt about ignoring the Madam was broken a moment later when I heard the Child's giggle from another direction.

In pursuit of that persistent giggle and the imitation of the clock, I chased the Child all over the house, never yet seeing him or even hearing the patter of his footsteps. I want to say that it took hours, but I really have no idea of how much time had passed, despite the ever present ticking of the clock and the Child's poor impression of the device.

Eventually the Child's calls led me right back to the study wherein I first heard him. Outside in the hall, the Madam was helpfully pointing at the study's door, but I already knew the boy was within.

As I slowly opened the door, pushing past the agonizingly sharp creak the door made, I scanned the room. I noticed the Butler first, as he stood flat against the wall opposite the door. Next I saw the Madam, pointing once again helpfully at the desk. In my comfortable chair behind the desk crouched the Child.

He was a boy of just a few years. Though I was myself childless and not good at judging children's ages, I expected he would be around five or six years of age. His hair was a sandy brown. He wore short pants and a white shirt stained by days of play. He half-sat, half-crouched in my chair, his knees pulled up against his chest, his palms flat on the chair as if to launch himself off at any moment. He wore a laughing grin and there was something in his eyes that made me wonder if even for his supposed age he might be a little slower than the other kids, perhaps even touched. Being a ghost, I had no idea how he measured against his peers.

"Tick tock, tick tock!" he said, then giggled, the sound higher pitched, as if squeezed from his throat with great force.

"Who are you?" I asked, but the response was unenlightening.

"Tick tock, tick tock!" said the Child. Pushing off from the chair, he ran around the room in a near complete circle. When he reached the door, he effortlessly passed by the Madam and myself. His diminutive form was now let loose upon the entire house again.

I kept seeing the Child, but in no interaction did he react in any way other than what I have recounted. His words were always the same, his giggle always high pitched and choked. He might run, he might change position, but in no way did he try to interact rather than laughing. Ultimately the Madam's silent pointing was of more use than the Child.

4

When it was just the Butler and the Madam, I had yearned for them to speak and communicate what seemed lost. But after the arrival of the Child and the Countess I longed for the silence when there were only two ghosts!

Whereas the Child echoed the ticking of the ubiquitous grandfather clock, the Countess at first seemed to be counting the hours, though I wondered if she had ever completed her counting. She always stopped too soon.

"One... two... three... *four*..."

Her words were not those of anticipation, nor was she flatly counting each number before proceeding to the next. No, there was great emotion in each number she stated. When she said *one* her voice was that of choked shock curdled with fear. With the count of *two* the fear was rising and the shock giving way. By the count of *three* shock had vanished and had been replaced with revulsion. By *four*, her voice was choked and dying on her throat as horror had completely overtaken her.

She was an older woman, her face lined with the years. As she counted, her voice descended from shock to horror like her words. There was such confusion on her face. One could almost read just how she couldn't fathom what she was seeing or counting. Yet she never made it to five. She went from one through four, a halting pause between each. But five never arrived, as if her voice vanished before she could make it. As she approached five, she was silent, her face contorted in emotion.

I do not know what it was that caused her to begin counting again. I had not noticed a particular interval between her counts. She would stop and then sometime later the count happened again, an increasing crescendo of disturbed emotions. There was nowhere in this house I could hide from it; no matter how low her voice sounded, it reached me in any room.

The Countess did not seem to be aware of me. Or rather, she did not react to me. She often looked at me as she counted, but there was no change in her no matter what I did. Her behavior seemed to be locked, much like the Madam or the Butler. And so her continual counting was a disturbing annoyance. I wished she had never come.

"One... two... three... *four*..."

5

The grandfather clock struck the hour, its bonging echoing through the house. The sound was loud, reverberating through the halls and unimpeded by the walls. It seemed so much stronger than I recalled. I began wondering if it was louder than usual or if it had just been so long since it had last rung.

I tried to keep working on the estate, but the bonging of the clock was so loud and it rattled my nerves. All I could hear was the incessant noise ringing in my ears and making my head throb. But it seemed I was not the only one affected. The room was suddenly full of all four ghosts. The Butler had been here already, as he always was. If the Madam had been here before, she had not made her presence known to me. Now she stood in front of my desk, her body turned and rigidly pointing at the door. The Child sat on the floor rocking back and forth, his *tick tocks* almost drowned out by the clock. The Countess was again counting. For a moment I wondered if she was counting the rings of the grandfather clock, but after a few moments watching I realized that the timing wasn't right.

I threw down my pen in frustration. As if in reaction, the candlestick holder fell to the ground again, but I ignored it. The noise was too great for me to concentrate and for some reason, it felt like the clock was going on far longer than it should. I knew I couldn't wait out this disruption. I rose from my chair and went out in the hall, intending to right the clock which was obviously malfunctioning.

As I passed through the door, I found the Madam in front of me. She was at the railing pointing down at the grandfather clock. The Butler was of course present. The Child burst from the doorway behind me and ran down the stairs while giggling. The Countess continued her enumeration but I ignored her and descended the steps.

The infernal noise was naturally greater right in front of the clock. Its gilded face stared at me. Its hands were set at 5 o'clock, yet it had definitely been striking more than five times for the hour. I wondered if the mechanism had caught. I opened the glass door to examine the chains.

As if I had opened a door to outside, a chill wind rushed past me from within the clock. Involuntarily I took a step back. I looked inside the clock and noticed a darkness from within. I wondered if it was just my eyes or a trick of the light, but it was as if a shadow was expanding from within the clock. In a moment that darkness stepped out, a man-sized shadow that seemed to solidify in front of me.

I reeled in terror, pulling back, but I found that my legs were frozen in position. The dark shadow reared up, becoming twice its height, its long arms reaching toward me. I wished to flee, to recoil from this new terror, but none of my limbs responded and I stood in abject terror before it as those shadowy arms moved toward me, long fingers extending ever farther at me.

When they touched my shoulders, a chill numbness ran through my body, descending through my chest, as if those icy fingers clutched directly at my heart. I found myself shivering quite involuntarily. Fear had gripped me stronger than any emotion I had ever felt in my life.

That dark specter leaned toward me. I saw that shadowy head take on form, the darkness rendering itself into something which resembled a man's skull, though it lacked all the details of the real thing. But unlike the dead, unmoving bones of the dearly departed, this skull moved. Its socketed eyes seem to contract to show emotion and the jaw opened in speech.

Out of its mouth erupted a breath like the grave, a hissing draught of air stale with the cold peace of those condemned to their final rest. In those words I saw an endless cessation of life, a thousand gravestones, a mountain of skulls, and the cold blackness that exists beyond this short span we call a lifetime. In that sound I saw rot, not the fetid diseased rot of plague, but the dry, gnawing rot of inevitable decay, the dust of a million men reduced to nothing.

The words themselves chilled me to the bone, yet I must confess it was actually just a single word stretched out into multiple syllables. *"Juuudgggge... meeeeennnnttttt..."*

When this specter's voice finally ended, disappearing into the void from whence it had come, there was just a moment of cold silence, of unmoving frigid stillness. Then it spoke again.

"Cooooommmmmeee..."

"I... don't want to go anywhere with you..." I pleaded, somehow finding my voice even though my soul lingered on the precipice of terror.

There was no response from my grave-born inquisitor. Instead, its skull-like countenance simply stared at me and there rose something like an arctic breeze, ice born upon the strongest wind, a cold dampness that chilled all bones and changed all good feelings to despair.

And then everything changed.

How to find words to describe the transmigration of a poor soul into the unknown, of a doomed man cast into lost territories? Normal men are not equipped to describe the far reaching madness of the true nature of the cosmos, and I have always been a very normal man. Have you ever had such a difficulty disrobing in the absence of servants that quite accidentally you inverted your clothing, the arms of the garment reversing from inside to outside, everything turned contrary to how they were intended? Then consider the world, everything I knew, everything around that grandfather clock I stood before, all turning as contrary as those garments. It did not all go black, it simply contracted and twisted, then finally expanding and dilating into something different, something new. I myself seemed to go through this same jarring and revolting process, an uncomfortable nausea rising up within me, threatening my bowels and humors, yet there was no vomitous eruption. Whatever sickness was within me, it was resigned to stay inside, churning through my innards.

And when it was all over, I found myself elsewhere.

6

Elsewhere was both an accurate and an inaccurate term for where I found myself after the encounter with the dark specter. I was not where I had been before that encounter; I was now in a wholly new place that I had never been before. And yet, this place that I found myself was familiar in many ways. Though the layout of this strange place was unknown to me, the walls of it were known to me, because they were the walls of the house I had just been in, the one I grew up in.

The walls were the same material, the same color. They were even covered with family pictures. These were without a doubt my family; I recognized all these images. And yet, these were changed from what I knew. The eyes of all were sightless; where a normal person would have eyes there were just white sockets. It was as if my entire family line had been blighted with a disturbing blindness in every depiction. And the expressions in the pictures were changed. Where once there were stoic respectfulness or the occasional smile, now there was impassive apathy or outright disgust. It was subtle and disturbing, seeing the same images that were familiar through my entire lifetime changed to cruel mockeries.

Within this place the ticking of the grandfather clock was still obvious. If anything, the tick was louder and stronger, echoing through this place as if it were this otherworld's heartbeat. Besides the increase in volume, something was off in the sound, causing me to continually think I should go wind the clock. Yet it was not the sound of time winding down. It was instead a strange echo or a muffling, a distortion of the original sound into a new form, an alien yet familiar tick that was the true inhabitant of these halls.

I was alone here. I saw none of the familiar ghosts. The Butler was absent, the Madam did not point, the Child did not laugh, the Countess did not count. I at first found this a relief. But as time stretched I found it a curse. I was alone.

This place corresponded to no reasonable layout of a house. It was a labyrinthine collection of halls and corridors. If anything, these strangely twisting and sometimes cramped hallways seemed like they were more likely the spaces *between* the halls of a mansion, as if I now was somewhere within the walls, running confusedly like a rat in the burrowed warrens inside my own house. This was of course preposterous, considering these halls were furnished and decorated. But the structure of these halls still made no sense as I wandered them seeking anything that would explain them or at least let me escape their clutches.

This is also where the blood returned. Now I didn't need to lift the pictures to see the blood. Now I saw it dripping down from behind the frames and staining the walls. First I saw it on a single picture. It looked exactly as I had seen it before - a single tear drop of blood on a lonely dissent. Because it was so similar, so exactly the same in appearance as the last time, I walked by it, my step hastening, trying to ignore the repeated phenomenon. A turn around a corner and then I saw that there were two picture frames bleeding. The blood drops were exactly the same, perfect twins. My pace quickening, I went on to another corridor - and saw more blood. This time I ran. Each turn I took, each hallway I turned down, I saw the same, blood, blood everywhere, increasing with every corner. Eventually every frame in the hall was bleeding. The same drop descended from every picture in the same way.

Panting, I finally came to a halt. I did not want to admit that it was inescapable; some part of me still felt if I ran far enough or fast enough, I would make my escape. But my legs and my curiosity betrayed me - the vigor had left my limbs for now and I wanted to know why. Why were the pictures bleeding?

I picked up the nearest frame from the wall, grabbing at a picture of my mother, ignoring the white, sightless eyes that stared at me. Removing it from the wall had me recoil in shock, as the blood did not drip from the frame's hook as before, but from a sentence written in blood behind the picture.

SONS SHOULD LOVE THEIR MOTHERS

I grabbed at another frame on the wall, practically tearing it from the hook and dropping it on the ground.

SONS SHOULD LOVE THEIR MOTHERS

I found myself in a frenzy, grabbing at frames and tossing them aside, revealing the same message over and over.

SONS SHOULD LOVE THEIR MOTHERS SONS SHOULD LOVE THEIR MOTHERS SONS SHOULD LOVE THEIR MOTHERS SONS SHOULD LOVE THEIR MOTHERS

What did it mean? Why was it there?

I was so engrossed in the panic that came from revealing the phrase and trying to understand its meaning, that I was completely surprised when I turned my head to find a pale and intense face just inches from mine.

It was the Countess. But she was not counting. Her eyes were wide, her jaw almost gaping. Her face was covered with shock, disbelief, and a small smattering of reproach.

"What have you done?" she said, her voice choked to a screech at the end.

"I... I didn't do this!" I said defensively.

"What have you done?" she repeated, her voice exactly the same as before.

"I didn't do this!" I screamed.

"What have you done?"

I clutched my head, the ticking of the grandfather clock echoing in the halls so much louder, almost as strong as when it struck the hour. It vibrated through my ears, rattling ever part of me.

"What have you done?"

My feet found the floor easier than my thoughts found their way. I ran, shrieking incomprehensible defenses to the Countess's question, running for an escape down these endless halls and countless corners. I know not how long or how far I ran, only that I did not stop until I had exhausted my shame and confusion, my fear and my evasion. Only when I felt far enough away to once again put up the illusion of safety and denial did I stop.

7

I don't know how long I travelled in that labyrinth. Minutes, hours, days, weeks, months? Time had lost its meaning to me. I heard the incessant ticking through the halls, not marking the moments as they passed, but seeming to chip away at them, turning the seconds into a sprawling mad thread which kept these halls together into something cohesive. I walked as a man stripped of purpose. Though all my hopes still lay with escape, that hope had long ago been smothered and reduced to a far off dream, an Elfland wonder unreachable by mortal hands. Whether I admitted it or not, I had resigned myself to these endless halls, no longer looking for an exit or an end, instead just refusing to stop, denying rest and stillness. I walked like an automaton, endlessly and without thought.

The walls bled. Every wall, every frame, in every hall. They all bled. That one long, lingering teardrop of blood. It never reached the floor; none of them ever reached the floor. Though they always appeared to be moving, they never met their destination. I had tried watching one until my patience ran out. Then I turned my head to look at another. When I looked back, that first was back to a higher point on the wall, dribbling a surface now unstained by its previous path. I blinked my eyes in disbelief, realizing this added up with all the other madness I experienced. I was waiting on a moment that was never going to arrive. Or holding onto a moment I would never give up.

I thought of the dark specter from the clock again. I thought of that tomb-like rest it had suggested. Then I remembered the coldness, the darkness, the endless respite. For a second, just a single second, I felt like that could be sufficient. I would like that.

My head slammed against a door. I had not even realized that my legs had surged into emotion again, my thoughts distracted and my consciousness so ragged at this point. I know not the route by which I came here, only that I arrived at the first door I had seen in this place.

As the walls were familiar elements from our house, so was the door. I knew this door well. It was the portal to Mother's sitting room, long closed off and taboo while I worked on the family's estate. Its very existence in this place made me step back as if struck. Then I saw what was written on the door in blood.

I'm sorry.

Though written in blood, these words were obviously not intended to be read emphatically like the other words I had seen. Something about these words were soft. Apologetic. Sorrowful. Receding.

I recognized the handwriting. It was the same hand that had written it in dust on the front of the picture in the hallway of the house so long ago. Here the text was larger and etched in blood, but the similarity was unmistakable.

My hand hovered in air, paused in the action of reaching for the door. Had my hand reached out automatically and I consciously stopped myself, or had I reached out consciously and some automatic movement stopped me? My hand shook and wavered in the air, as if a pawn of some fell magnetism on the part of the door handle. The door itself instilled in me a cold, overwhelming fear. I knew not why, but at this point I knew not my own mind. An eternity in these halls had stripped me of everything I knew. I just counted myself lucky I had not yet encountered the Countess and her accusations again.

Looking on with horror at the rebellious nature of my hand as it twisted the handle of the door, my decision was made for me. I pushed the door open. Suddenly the ever present grandfather clock struck the hour. The bong sound vibrated through everything, shaking the halls, my ears throbbing with pain, my body stumbling as if there was a tremor. The brief moment between that sound and its next succession gave no respite, just a single second of a frantic grasp at righting myself before the next assault came. Five times the grandfather clock struck, five times to strike the hour before the sound receded back into ticking.

I found myself sprawled on the floor of Mother's sitting room, fear leaping through my whole body, some denial stretching through me, fighting off a sense of déjà vu as I looked at the candlestick holder on the floor.

Above me stood Mother. She was dressed as I last knew her, in one of her favorite dresses, the one I asked her to wear when she first met Joanna. She seemed taller than she ever was, but maybe that was because I was sprawled on the ground.

"Help me, Mother," I said, barely finding any voice to even ask.

Her face was a mask of anger, a rage she never showed anyone except in rare cases. Other than when the mask slipped, I had only seen this rage before once...

"Sons should love their mothers!" she spat at me, her anger ill-concealed.

"What?"

"Sons should love their mothers!"

"I've always loved you, Mother!"

"Sons should love their mothers!" More insistent, more rage.

"I love you, Mother!"

"Sons should love their mothers!" Louder. Her rage was now frothing.

The candlestick holder fell to the floor loudly and rolled across the room. When had it been picked off the floor?

"I've always loved you, Mother, but I have my own life to live!"

Her face showed shock. "Sons should love their mothers!"

"It's you who have never loved me! *And you don't want me to go live with Joanna!*"

Her mouth opened, but no sound came out. The grandfather clock began bonging again. The candlestick dropped loudly to the floor. "What have you done?" said someone. Laughter, counting, shock, and the ticking of a clock.

Pieces of a broken mirror, suddenly reformed in a moment shadowed by a dark specter.

I remembered.

8

I had denied the moment so long that now it ripped through me like shards of glass. But there was also relief. I didn't have to live a lie again, fighting against myself. I didn't have to ignore the pain. I didn't have to pretend against the betrayal, claiming love was stronger than darkness. It wasn't love. She didn't love me. She controlled me.

No more ghosts. Just the truth.

I had returned home from seeing Joanna. We had talked it all over. She had agreed to my proposal and our plans had been set. We would leave in two days time. It was the happiest day of my life. Mother wouldn't like it, but it was my life. I just hadn't told Mother yet.

I found Mother in her sitting room, as always, holding court like the decadent queen she wished she was. Today was a busy day for my mother's court. My aunt was here, as she was most days. But my sister had come to the house today as well, the first time in many months, bringing her insufferable little boy. James, our butler, attended to my mother as always.

Presenting myself, I asked for privacy to confer with Mother alone. She shooed them all with a flick of her wrist, preferring that the majority of those in the room find somewhere else to be than deign to move from her throne on the couch I've always hated.

Once we were alone, I told her of my intentions. Joanna and I were to be married. We'd travel to Paris in two days time and begin our life together. I carefully explained that I had already proposed and Joanna had said yes. My decision could not be changed.

Anger struck my mother. She asked why she hadn't been informed, why she wasn't part of the decision. I had purposely not included her because she would have said no. She would keep me here in this house, this prison for my whole life, claiming she needed me. Even then I realized the control she had over me, a control she thrived on. Joanna was my escape. In hindsight I only wish we had left without a word instead of doing Mother the courtesy of telling her in advance.

"Don't you love me?" she said. "You will leave me here alone and uncared for?"

"James is the one who does everything around the house!" I countered. "I do nothing! And Aunt Miriam is here every day!"

"You cover the finances," she said, a loose lie. I make the figures work, but she makes all the decisions. The work is just delegated to me.

"Agatha's husband is a banker, surely he'd have no trouble with his Mother-in-Law's finances."

"You don't love me!" she decided petulantly.

"Of course I do," I said, "but I need to live my life!"

"You don't love me," she said, her bulk rising from the couch in anger. "Sons should love their mothers!"

"I love you, Mother, but Joanna and I will be married!"

"I am the only one who will ever love you," she said. "And you throw that all away!"

"I love Joanna and she loves me! You will see that one day!"

"You will not stay under this roof if that's your decision," she said venomously. "If you choose that harlot over me, you are never again welcome here!"

"Fine!" I said in anger. "I'll leave today then! You'll never see me again!"

I turned to leave, such anger in me, wanting to leave the prison of this house and my mother's jealous grasp. It was nearly five o'clock. I knew that I could go to Joanna or still get lodgings at this hour.

"You can't leave! Sons should love their mothers!" I heard bellowed from behind me. I turned just in time to see my mother rush toward me, holding a candlestick holder in her hand. I raised my arms in defense, but it was too late. She swung the heavy object.

Incredible pain blossomed in my head. I barely understand what happened outside the red pain that seared through me. I think I was on the ground. But then red, horrible pain burst through me again as she hit me a second time. Then the world fell apart as she hit me a third time, my ears vaguely aware of an ugly meat sound. On the fourth strike I began to forget who I was, just vaguely aware of another world that existed through my open eyes.

She stood before me, her face fading from anger to horror and grief. She held onto the candlestick. My eyes were drawn to that and the single drop of blood which dripped from it, lingering in the air but never reaching the ground.

Then she turned away from me, sobbing. The candlestick holder fell from her hand, hitting the floor with a loud noise before rolling to hit my foot.

"I'm sorry," sobbed my mother.

The noise had attracted others to the room. My dying eyes had a view of the door as it opened. My aunt came into the room, her face covered with shock. "What have you done?"

The grandfather clock began striking the hour. Five o'clock.

Horror began crossing my aunt's face. She looked over each of my wounds. "One, two, three... *four?*" She counted each strike my mother had given me, disbelief and revulsion rushing in.

My nephew came running into the room, seeming to have just escaped whichever adult was holding him still despite his endless enthusiasm. Already a strangely touched child, he did not react to my bloody body. He simply remarked on the clock. "Tick tock, tick tock!" Then he laughed.

His mother, my sister, ran into the room, first seeking to keep him from disrupting, but then she saw the mess in front of her. In her own shock, she only pointed at the collapsed heap that was my dying body, covered her face with her other hand, as if looking through her fingers would ward off the horror of it all.

Behind her appeared the butler, James. He simply looked. His whole life had been based on his polite and impassive mask. But in the face of this bloody crime, even that began to drop as emotion infected his face.

I took them all in, an endless moment frozen in time, one that would torment me due to my denial. Reliving it again, I understood it all. I understood that I was dead. I was the last ghost. I was the only ghost.

Where's the dark specter? I thought. I knew now that it was his job to take me away from all this. To take me to the great beyond.

The scene before me slowing to a halt, that dark shadowy man appeared in front of me. His skeletal jaw opened and once again came the voice of a thousand years in the grave, his breath the stench of a thousand souls in a void.

"*Time to go...*" His voice was no longer slow or difficult. Before there was a chasm between us. Now I understood him clearly.

I nodded.

"*You belong to me now...*"

"I understand," I said, finally truly understanding. But even in that acceptance, there was a twinge of regret. There was one last bit of my humanity that clung to the life which had passed, lighting a spark of hope against the all encompassing darkness. "I know I'm no longer of this world anymore. But I have one last request." I paused. "Can... can I see my beloved, my Joanna, just one more time? I want to see her one more time, even if she cannot see me. I want to hold her image with me until the end of eternity."

The response came with the cold chill of the endless grave, of the loneliness of an eternity that yawned before me in an empty void.

"*No.*"

Confession to a Friend

1

I need your help. I've gone over this in my head a thousand times, but I don't know how better to tell you this. You're a good friend, so I think you're the only person I can tell this to. You need to promise not to freak out. You need to promise not to tell anyone. I need to tell you this, I need to tell someone this before I go crazy. Maybe crazier.

I don't know if you remember, but I went on a vacation recently. One of those find-yourself trips across America by motorcycle. I'm not sure I like the me I found out there. The whole trip did not work out the way I planned. It fell apart... and things happened. Well, let me be straight with you.

I think I killed somebody out there.

Yeah.

It happened, okay? It just happened. I didn't intend to, it just happened.

But listen, I don't think anybody found the body. It happened out in the desert. It was somewhere in New Mexico, and that's all I'm going to say about the location right now. Just hear me out first? I need someone to just listen to me, and maybe we can figure this out.

It was supposed to be a simple trip. One of those manly trips to free out spirits, to get away from the nine to five grind of society. It was supposed to be true freedom, just ourselves and the open road, communing with the spirit of America like Easy Rider or something.

Yes, I know that film was made over forty years ago. Yeah, I know someone else died in that too.

Something was very appealing about the Southwest. Dusty roads, an absence of anything at all, and that big huge sky above us. I liked the idea that we'd be going town to town across the borderlands like cowboys or something. It was also a better area to find territory to find peyote, which was something I really wanted to try. At the very least, Ted swore he knew where to get some awesome mushrooms.

Ted was the guy I travelled with, and kind of my guide for this whole adventure. He had rode this path the year before. I'll admit he talked me into. He had been hounding me for weeks about how I needed to "find my true spirit among the mystic places of the American Southwest". I'm pretty sure he hadn't intended for it to work out this way.

Ted was... well, he wasn't a friend. Not if I'm being entirely truthful. It's not like we were enemies or anything, we were just more acquaintances. We knew each other through work, though we didn't work directly with each other.

We weren't friends because, well... Ted pissed people off. Myself included. He was always such a know it all about things. And he had this incredible arrogance about his "free spirited" nature, his pro-drug lifestyle, and how he "plumbed the depths of consciousness". It's like he didn't go to work at the same shitty office as me to get a paycheck so he could make rent, as if the fact he took mushrooms and shamanic journeys on the weekends made him better than me.

I'll admit that maybe I was a little jealous. Maybe I wished I could be more relaxed at work, to take it less seriously, and to get into all the same Terrence McKenna drug shit that he did. But I hadn't and always held myself back. That was still no excuse for him to be so goddamn pretentious about it.

Now that I think about it, I wonder why he wanted me to go. We weren't friends and I hadn't been as into stuff as everything. Yet he kept nagging me to go and it seemed a victory when I agreed. What did it matter if I went? Why did he want me to come along?

Whatever our reasons for the trip and companionship, when the appointed day came, we left. Without second guessing myself, I suited up, gunned the motor and rode out of town with him, looking for my destiny and finding something very different.

We rode from Austin to El Paso and then into New Mexico. Ultimately we were to push on through Arizona and finally to San Diego. It was a long ride, but there was something about being on that bike, the road stretched out endlessly in front of me, that was almost meditative. My job, my cramped life, my friends, and all my worries were left behind me so my obligations and tensions were slowly peeled away from me the farther we got from home. I felt like I was becoming more myself. Maybe my problem is I don't like the me I found.

We followed Ted's route from last year exactly. We stopped each night at the same location he had stayed, even if we could have made better time and gone faster. I was not in a hurry and was okay with letting someone else make the decisions. The specific stop offs gave the trip an air of pilgrimage, each of his previous stops like a way station.

We camped every night. Warming our bodies by the fire, Ted said that the stars and the sky were better friends to our spirits. He suggested that man made buildings sap our spirits and ensnare us.

I have to admit it was all so beautiful. Whether seen from great speed on a motorcycle or stared at lazily over a can of beans around the fire, New Mexico was beautiful. It felt good to have time to myself; I had not realized how much my job dominated my life, even after the work day was over. I told myself that I was beginning to feel free, like I what I thought Ted must feel. At least, this is felt like what he always bragged about.

Almost every evening also involved a shared joint that we smoked while we stared at the sky. It helped me appreciate the sounds and beauty of nature. My placid enjoyment was only marred by Ted saying that this was nothing compared to taking shrooms and tripping out in the open desert. He said that feeling was shamanic and would truly connect our souls to the spirit of the Southwest. He went on to say it was "real mystic", looking straight at me when he said that. Moments later he started babbling on about how we would become shamanic warriors, and I zoned out. Some of his ideas were real out there, and I've never been big on long involved conversations when I'm stoned.

The days were fun and nothing would have made me guess things were going to sour. During the day we raced down the roads, slowing only when Ted got paranoid of police traps. I followed his lead. While I was beginning to relax, Ted seemed to be getting more amped up. No matter where we went, Ted had to be the fastest and first, while I just enjoyed the journey the scenery. It was a liberated feeling that was too brief.

We stopped at this little town in the middle of nothing. Granted, a whole lot of New Mexico is like that, but I didn't even get the name of this town. It was one road, a few buildings, and a few rickety stands of people selling souvenirs. I'm not even sure who they expected to sell those to.

"I have to pick up something," said Ted. "Wait here, I don't want to spook my friend."

The shop seemed to sell Native American trinkets and souvenirs, things like dream catchers, animal skulls, and objects with snake fangs or engraved horns. It looked like there were peace pipes, feathered clothing, and small resin statues too. Maybe it had more, but that's all I could see in the window.

It was obvious to me that this visit was about drugs, but Ted wouldn't say anything about it. When he was paranoid, he didn't even want to mention drugs, he just talked around the subject. He came out a few minutes later with a nervous smile and a quick look over his should.

"Got it," he said. We rode off.

I found out later that what he had picked up were the "good" mushrooms that I had heard so much about. Of course now I know that whatever he got was just pure fucking concentrated evil. I wish I had never taken those fucking things. I wished I had turned back towards Austin or kept on riding to Arizona and left Ted and his "medicine" far behind.

Yes, he called them medicine. He said natural psychedelics like mushrooms and peyote were healing medicine that repair the link between a man and his spirit, as well as the link between that spirit and the earth. According to him, synthetic drugs like acid might be similar, but they harmed the mind and the spirit. It had to be natural medicine like mushrooms to cure your ailments. He said the Native Americans had been doing this shit for centuries.

We just "had to" do the shrooms at the same place that he had done them last year. He said the experience had been unforgettable and had changed his life forever. We had to do it the same way. He was adamant about this place and refused to discuss elsewhere. It was in the middle of nowhere out in the desert, a bigger middle of nowhere than we had camped in before, so I asked about it. It's not like I had a better idea of where to take the mushrooms, but it was strange that he was so forceful about this point. His responses if I questioned him were defensive.

"Stop being such a fucking pussy, man," he said. "You've been living in a cubicle for too long that you're like an insect in their hive. To meet the spirit of the land, you need to take some fucking risks. I'm fucking going to the place and that's where I'm going to have my experience. If you don't want to come, fine, but I'm taking the fucking shrooms with me."

I'm sure I could have turned around and gone home, but at the time, there didn't seem a reason to split up. We began the trip together, we might as well finish it together. I *did* want to try the mushrooms and I had never tripped in the middle of nowhere, so there was some appeal. So despite the hissy fit he threw, I finally agreed. He smiled and asked me to follow him.

At a gnarled tree at the edge of the road he signaled. This spot didn't look any different from any other except for the tree. I looked at the tree. It was dead and leafless but had not fallen apart. I saw that someone had left some things hanging from the branches. Strings with snake fangs and a small animal skull. Weird, for sure, but I had not realized that this was the signpost of madness. Instead I simply shrugged and followed him as we turned off the road and went into the rough parched ground of the desert.

This is where things started getting fucked up. I should have kept on riding. I should have taken one look at the tree and told him to fuck off. Things would have been better that way. Sure, I wouldn't have been able to call myself an adventurer, but I would have had to call myself a murderer instead. Shit, am I a murderer? I don't even know at this point.

2

The camping spot was right at the ground transition of dusty dirt and sheets of rock. Farther away were greater collections of rocks erupting from the ground like sharp hills or small mountains. A gnarled tree had once grown here, twisting up to the sky, but it had fallen, now curving and sprawled across the ground. This was his second landmark for finding the spot.

It was growing dark when we found it, so we quickly found some kindling for the fire, though we were both exhausted. Ted got the fire going and we cooked ourselves some food from our cans. Ted said we needed to eat a little bit before the mushrooms so we don't throw up, but not too much. If we overdid it and we wouldn't get the full effect. He also said we wouldn't want to eat while on them. Then he went off on this story about this one time he was tripping hardcore, and he made the mistake of trying to eat some canned soup, which he found horrifying. He even laughed at his own stories, despite the fact I wasn't paying attention. My patience with him had been thinning over this trip.

After eating, we waited about a half an hour during which he babbled about how awesome everything was going to be. Then he pulled out the mushrooms. They were in a plastic zip lock bag, with a little bit of a dark liquid sloshing around. He explained that was there to keep them fresh and that you trip so much harder than the dried mushrooms. He took some himself, the handed the bag over to me.

They tasted like ass. They tasted more like dirt than anything else. I want to say they tasted funny, but I had never done mushrooms before, so I had no idea what they should taste like. A minute later and I regretted eating anything at all. My stomach churned. I thought of my childhood science project, the volcano made with baking powder and vinegar. My stomach growled, and I swear it sounded more like something boiling than an actual growl. Ted heard it and laughed at me, calling me a 'lightweight'.

Over the next few minutes, my stomach felt really bad, and the churning never stopped. I kept swallowing more saliva and making grimacing facial expressions, as if that would somehow help my stomach make up its mind. I worried if I would throw up. Ted noticed my continued discomfort and dropped his amused expression. "Keep 'em down, pussy, that's some expensive shit, and I won't have you yakking them up on the ground." I wanted to puke all over him when he said that, but I wasn't interested in vomiting either. I finally mastered them and while my stomach was still unsettled, I didn't have an urgent fear of puking my guts out.

A few minutes later, my stomach felt more like it was willing to play ball. It still felt a little funny down in the pit of it, but the rest of it was not doing jumping jacks anymore, so I counted this as a major plus. Ted had pulled out a bottle of cheap wine he picked up in town. He was taking large gulps of the wine every so often, while expounding on the manliness of sleeping under the stars, as well as hunting your own food in nature. The empty can of Cap'n Marsh's Tasty Tuna next to him had no comment.

As I said, I had never done mushrooms before, so I was not sure quite what to expect. I've done acid before, so I was ready for those unsafe-in-my-own-skin feelings, tinged colors, and that general feeling of the world turning almost sugary in its pleasantness. It turns out that mushrooms are not as similar to acid as I had heard. Then again, I'm still not entirely sure these were mushrooms. They may have been... fuck. I'm getting ahead of myself. Whatever I was feeling was unfamiliar and unpleasant. Not the best start.

My thoughts were interrupted by the wine bottle being thrust in my face. My stomach was still unsettled, but for some reason the wine was still appealing. I took a drink, a big gulp, since I knew faltering or pushing it away would just produce more criticism from Ted. It was white wine, or maybe piss with some beer poured into it. Tasted like crap, went down like crap, sat in my stomach like crap. "Ugh, don't give me this fucking shit," I said as I tossed the bottle at him.

He laughed, then started into some story about something. His words just faded into background noise. The crappy wine made my stomach churn a little. I burped, which was a mistake as it smelled horrible and tasted even worse. My solar plexus felt tight and tingly, which I hadn't really ever felt before. I was clearly feeling strange, but I wasn't sure if that was from the actual effects of the mushrooms or from getting sick. I was beginning to feel dizzy, so I rubbed my eyes for a moment, but that didn't help.

Ted was still talking. I spent most of my time staring at the fire. It drew my attention away from my sick and strange feelings. My arms began to feel light and floaty. When I turned to look up at the full moon, I realized I was gritting my teeth for some reason. I did like the moon's glow on the clear sky out here away from it all. Despite my weird feelings, I did appreciate how great it was to not be slave to a clock back at home and my job.

"Hey," Ted said, trying to grab my attention. He was looking right at me. Generally if he had something important to say, he would look right at me. When he talked about random crap, he tended to look around or away, as if he knew in the back of his mind that no one fucking cared. I rarely cared, so I had a nice cue for when I could zone out. "Last year, I stayed here too," he said.

"Yeah," I said, my voice slower than intended, "you told me."

"It was on this very spot that I ate some mushrooms."

"Yeah, that too."

"What I didn't tell you is this spot is special. I didn't know that when I was here the first time. Doesn't it feel special?"

I turned my head and looked around. My head was light, so turning it was somewhat disorienting I felt myself shiver a bit, but I wasn't cold. My solar plexus tingled. But I didn't see anything different around us. There didn't seem a damn thing special about this spot.

"There's something here," he said, probably not even listening to me. "Something old. I'm sure you can feel it. Here in the ground. I felt it last time. I more than felt it."

He paused and took a gulp of wine, letting me sit there a moment or two wondering. Only some of it was wondering about his story, the rest of it was wondering if I should care.

"It came to me while I was on the mushrooms," he continued. "Straight out of the ground, because it is the ground. It's all around here in the Southwest, its energy twists around things. Some say it *is* the Southwest." If that doesn't make sense to you, then we're on the same page.

He paused again, breaking eye contact, and smiled to himself as he held the bottle. After a moment he resumed his bleak expression. I remember looking at the expression and wondering why he looked so odd. He looked... nervous.

"It was the Snake God," said Ted. "It waits under the earth. For the right people, I guess. It wanted me, it wanted to talk to me. It's like... this unfathomable darkness. Like being so deep in a cavern that sunlight has never shown. It's a dark force and it's indifferent. It doesn't care whether humanity lives or dies. It just waits."

I admit, his words were having an effect on me. While I had grown tired of Ted's crap, there was something eerie about this. Something about the drugs and the situation had me picking up on his nervousness. There was a prickling of hairs on the back of my neck.

"You see, it came and told me..." He trailed off, looking into space again. His hand drifted over to the wine bottle and held it. He smiled and gave a little laugh. "I'm sorry, man, I'm just fucking with you." He then took a drink from the bottle.

I was fucking pissed, but that's just the kind of ass he was. I knew a guy like that in college, the kind that likes to fuck with people when they're stoned. It's something I hate in general, but when in the middle of nowhere, doing shrooms for the first time, and with someone I was beginning to distrust, it was particularly uncool to start fucking with me.

"Asshole," I said, still shivering but not from the cold.

He laughed more and started talking random shit again, like how Native Americans sold iceboxes to Eskimos made out of hemp or something equally as pointless. I was annoyed with him and feeling strange, so the last thing I wanted to do was listen to him. I couldn't stop shivering. I still had my leather jacket on, but it didn't help.

As I looked up at the sky, I realized that somehow I felt bigger. The stars seemed closer, the moon just out of grasp. I looked around and saw that it seemed like our whole campsite had grown to titanic size, but everything was in perfect proportion so that it looked exactly the same.

I wanted to stand up and measure my new height against the height of those huge rocks near us, but thought better of it and stayed sitting. Besides, with the lightness of my body, it took a different kind of effort to move. I didn't feel like I moved my arms with muscles, I moved them with something else - I'd say willpower, but I was feeling a little too frazzled to say I really had willpower.

He turned to me again. "Are you feeling it?"

I looked up from my numb hand, which was flopping on the ground, surely at some enormous size. "Yeah, I think so."

"Yeah, me too." He paused. "When I trip, sometimes I don't feel like myself. Like I'm me, but something else too, y'know? Something's inside me. You ever feel like that?"

"Not particularly," I replied. My limbs might be falling dead to the floor, but they were still *my* limbs.

"It's like, I can feel something inside," he said. "Twisting around deep inside me. Whatever it is, it rises to the top when I trip. It's some weird force or consciousness that just bubbles up into me and takes over. Like possession or something."

Ted had that nervous look again. "Is it hitting you hard? It's hitting me totally fucking hard. I can almost see the words I'm saying."

"Not that hard," I responded, but I could see how reality was getting a bit more malleable.

"Yeah, so like this possession kind of grabs me. Fills me up inside. Makes me say stuff. And it feels like... Its dark and old, but it feels like..." He trailed off again.

"What does it feel like?" I said. I was curious, but also knew he would inevitably wait to be promoted.

"Like I am the earth, like I move through tunnels. I feel hungry... and I'm waiting, but still very hungry. I've been very hungry for a long, long time. Something needs to sate it. I'm the gaping maw of the earth. I've had my giant mouth open for a long period of time and nothing has satisfied my hunger."

"What the hell are you talking about?" I said. "You're not making any sense."

"A snake."

"What?"

"A snake," he said. "I'm a snake. I'm an extension of the snake that will eat the world. The earth will open up and I'll swallow humanity whole. I was there before humans, and I'll be here after they're gone. I am the land, and I've been waiting. Don't you see?"

I tried looking at him hard in the light of the fire. Was this really Ted? Or was he really possessed like he said? Was he just fucking with me? Was it all just the drugs and I was completely out of my mind.

As I squinted at him, I thought I could kind of see scales on him. Was that right? The longer I stared at him, the more that seemed right. His skin seemed darker. Was that a diamond pattern?

Was what he was saying true? He was a snake? How could he be a snake? We'd hung out a few times before this trip and he never before mentioned being a snake. It seemed like the sort of thing he'd bring up.

"I'm not sure what I'm seeing..." I said.

"I am older than humanity," he said, "A remnant from ages long past. And I've slept for so long. I've waited longer than any human lifespan. I know it will be time. My fangs will poison the world. When my hunger grows great enough, my waiting will end, my sleep will die, and it will be time."

Okay, he definitely had scales at this point. I'm not sure how I missed that fact beforehand. His eyes were all funny, more like an animal - I guess a snake's. When he spoke, I think I could see the fangs he was talking about. They got bigger the more I looked at them.

"I'm really not cool with this. Could we talk about something else?" I said. I really wanted to change the subject.

"My hunger is growing. See my fangs?" He opened his mouth wide, so now I could definitely see the fangs. His head didn't look human anymore. It was clearly a snake head, but somehow also Ted. "I need to devour. To eat, to destroy. I've slept so long..."

Before he simply looked at me, but now he was staring at me with those snake eyes and it was making me really uncomfortable. He was looking me up and down, and it felt like I could feel his stare on me. I shivered again. I really didn't want to be there. I wished he'd stop staring.

"Hey, man," I said. "I don't feel so good. I'm really not cool with things now."

He didn't act like he heard me.

Then things got even weirder.

I still don't believe it happened, but it did. I got the mark on my arm right here. I sat frozen as he leaned towards me. It was such a quick movement, yet I could see every part of it. He leaned forward and bit my left forearm.

It hurt. I screamed. He didn't tear my flesh away and the mushrooms had made me feel light and numb, but it still hurt and I was in shock.

After only a moment of shock and paralysis, I responded. "Ahhh, stop it, you fucker!" I shouted while punching him in the head repeatedly. After a second he pulled his head away. I hadn't done any real damage to him.

Ted smiled and then laughed. "I'm just fucking with you, man. You should totally see your face. That was fucking hilarious."

His head was still a snake. I didn't trust him.

I rubbed my arm as he kept laughing. There was a bruise and a little blood, but nothing serious, as far as I could tell. Meanwhile, he had started on some stupid story, as if he hadn't just bit my arm with his snake head. I was tense and began to realize how lethargic I was. It was probably the mushrooms. I also noticed how things sounded weird; not even my own voice sounded normal. The fire's ever-present crackling was distorted to sound almost like a snake rattle.

I looked him over, trying to figure out if I could take him in a fight. He already bit me once, so I was going to be prepared for round two. I decided I was bigger than him, but he spent more time camping, so he might be in better shape. Then again, he was drinking more, which would slow him down. I think the snake head made the most difference in my calculations. Those fangs were fucking big, and if he bit my neck or vein, I'd probably go down.

I then remembered I had a knife in my boot. I had never actually used it. I just remember when I bought these boots for this trip, that the knife in them looked really cool in the store. I had a fantasy of fighting against a sheriff with it after doing his daughter, or at least threatening hippies with it when they tried to mess with my stuff. Right now I tried to remember more about it. Was it on with Velcro, or was there a strap? How to be discreet and find out?

He was still talking about random shit. Right now he was telling about a girl he met and fucked while camping, and then she let him live at her place for a few months after that, with her paying all the bills. I think he talked to cover up his own nervousness, or due to some fantasy world he lived in. Both could be true, since I was realizing that he was a fucking delusional psycho who had me in the middle of nowhere.

I tried testing my drug addled reflexes, flexing my hand. As I looked at it, the movements were sluggish, but worse was that I couldn't quite feel the movement like I usually did. I felt like I felt the nerves of my hand but I didn't feel the flesh. There was a buzzing tingling sensation in the movement.

I think he might have seen me flexing. His babbling ceased abruptly. "These are some hardcore shrooms, aren't they? They aren't normally like this at all. These are special, do you know why?"

I tiredly repeated what he had told me incessantly before the trip. "You told me you knew this guy who grew them special in a building behind his home. Special facility or something. You said that makes them grow in crazy ways. And that these are the best because they really get you off."

He laughed. "Yeah, that's the shit I *told* you, man." He really emphasized the word "told", even sticking out his finger at me when he said it. After this, his amusement disappeared. "No, there's something more. Remember that guy at the shop, the one I got the shrooms from? He also serves the Snake God."

This sank in and seemed weird, yet impossible. I hadn't actually met the guy in the shop, so who knows what he was like. But surely this Snake God thing wasn't real and was just a big game, apart from the part where Ted had an actual snake head. But I was already more than paranoid and I felt a dull ache from the bite on my arm. Ted had gotten the shrooms without me because I wasn't allowed to come in. What had they talked about? Was that man coming here?

I whipped my head around, looking for some unknown assailant and did nothing but make myself dizzy and even more lightheaded.

"Do you want to know what he did to them?" said Ted, his voice buzzing across my consciousness like a swarm of angry bees.

I just nodded. I couldn't form words.

"These mushrooms have been soaked in snake venom. They're poisonous! Ha! Haven't you noticed that you're not exactly feeling right?"

My mind flashed back to the snake fangs I had seen outside the shop where Ted got the mushrooms. Could he have had the venom too? It was possible. But wait, there was something very obvious.

"You had the mushrooms too, so you would be poisoned too," I said. He had to be full of shit. He just *had* to be.

He smiled, a great, toothy snake smile. "Normally, that would be true. But when the Snake God chooses you, he gets inside of you. And once he's inside, you're full of his power. The fangs and venom of his children are meaningless against that. I won't be dying from poison."

He paused, letting this sink in. "So how are you feeling?" he said. "Is the venom getting to you? Do you feel it like ice in your veins?"

I was definitely not feeling good. I was still shivering, but I didn't feel cold. There wasn't any ice in my veins. That tingling feeling had been spreading up my arms and had now reached my shoulders. It wasn't ice, but could that be the poison? I reached up and rubbed my face. My own skin felt like a rubber mask. I learned I was sweating badly. My body was light, my head swirled, and dizziness had never left me.

"So how does it feel to die?" he said. "At least you die out here, away from all the chains of society. It's a full moon. It's a good night for rebirth. You're going to die out here in the wasteland. You'll be prepared for the next."

I couldn't take anymore. I was seriously freaked out. I needed to get away from there, to find some help, to do just *something*. I really wasn't sure what I would do, but I knew I had to get the hell away from him. I needed to be somewhere else.

It took a great deal of concerted effort, but I began to pull myself up. My body felt almost intangible, like I was controlling an image of myself, not something solid. Dizziness seared across me as inertia caused it to preferred my body to have stayed sitting. I finally reached a standing posture and was amazed my body could hold me up. I teetered for a second, but I had most of my balance. Ted was shocked I could move so well; it was written all over his snake face. Finally he spoke: "What are you doing?"

I didn't acknowledge him. I turned and began to walk or run or stumble as best as I could. It was more like falling forward, my legs constantly struggling to keep me standing. I ran into the darkness, leaving the fire behind me. I could vaguely tell I was running towards the rocks. I was running on hard ground and the surface was uneven.

I heard him call after me, panic and tension in his voice: "No! Don't go that way!"

I didn't listen and kept stumbling. I wanted to be away from him, but that didn't really work out how I wanted. My stumble turned into a trip, and then into a fall. I hit the ground for just a moment, because then I felt myself falling again. I thought the ground had just swallowed me up.

I was in darkness, the moon just vaguely visible above me. There were pebbles falling down around me. I had fallen somewhere. I was dizzy and my back was propped up against something hard.

I could vaguely hear footsteps. Then I heard Ted's voice. It seemed to come from above me, maybe five or ten feet. "Shit! Are you okay? Can you hear me? Answer me, tell me if you're okay!"

I didn't answer. I wasn't going to fucking answer him. It would be just what he wanted. It would make it easier for him to kill me. I sat down there in the darkness, just waiting, trying to not breathe loudly, even though my lungs wanted to gasp for air.

I heard him curse again. "Maybe you can hear me, but can't answer. Stay put, I'm going to get my flashlight and maybe see if we have some rope. Fuck!"

After a few seconds, I heard his footsteps move away and disappear. I knew I needed to figure out where I was. My body ached, but I managed to reach into my jacket and pull out my lighter. Good old expensive Zippo lighter. I had kept it around even when I stopped smoking years back.

Once I lit it, I could see there was rock in front of me and rock behind me. I seemed to be in some crevice or trench, a small crack in the earth. From what I could tell, it was about ten feet deep, and maybe two or three feet wide.

The rocks under my hands felt a bit weird, more smooth than rough. My eyes had trouble focusing, and what I could focus on tended to waver in the darkness. The rocks around me were strange. Were they really rocks? They looked almost like faces. I tried hard to focus on them. It was dark and covered in dirt, but was that... Was that... a skull? A human skull? I blinked, and tried to focus my eyes again.

It was a skull. It had to be a skull. It made sense. I looked around, trying to better look at things in the meager light. The smooth rocks, I realized were bone chips. I could see what looked like another skull a few feet to my left.

Now it all started to make sense. This was Ted's special spot. He really did intend to kill me. He would kill me and toss my body down here. That's why he brought me here, so he could easily dispose of the corpse. He gave me the venom first and then when I was weak, he'd strike.

He had done it before - that was obvious from the remains. Or maybe it wasn't even just him! There was the man from the shop! And there must be others who worshipped the Snake God. They needed to feed the god. And since the god was the earth itself... As my mind raced, it all fell into place. This was no normal crack in the earth. This was the Snake God's maw, its open mouth so its followers could throw sacrifices in it.

I knew I had to get out of there as soon as possible. But there was still the problem of Ted. I knew he waited only to kill me. He had the advantage. I was not only poisoned and tripping, but also hurt from my fall down here. I could try to stumble back to my bike and escape, but he had one too, so he could chase me down. We were in the middle of nowhere, so there was no help I could go for. It was a grim realization, but I knew that I would have to take him out.

I reached down and felt for the knife in my boot. It turned out that it was held on with Velcro. That single knife and the element of surprise were the only things I had going for me. I felt like shit, I was scared, I was poisoned, I was out of my mind, and I ached. But I knew if I were going to live, I would have to focus. I stood up. My left leg hurt a lot more than I thought. I started looking at the wall of the crevice as best I could to see how I could get out.

I heard footsteps returning. I closed my lighter and put it away. I tensed, ready for anything he might throw at me. I didn't have a lot of room to dodge. This was obviously not a good position for me.

I saw a light shine down the crevice from his flashlight. It hurt my eyes at first, but I adjusted. "You're awake! Thank god! Shit man, you had me fucking freaking out! I saw this hole last time I was here, and didn't know what the fuck I'd do if you were knocked out." He paused, waiting for a response, but when I didn't respond, he went on talking. "I couldn't find any rope. Maybe if I keep this shining down there, you can find a good place to climb or something. Can you walk?"

I didn't answer. It might seem like he was concerned, but it was a trick. He was just disarming me, lulling me into a docile state. And then he'd start up with his strange words again soon. Or he might decide it was time and just try to kill me. Either way, I was not going to give him that chance.

I started looking for a place to climb and found a place that was reasonable enough with my hurt leg. My hands still felt enormous and tingly, but somehow I pulled myself together enough to start climbing.

As I climbed, he started talking again. His hands were shaky as he held the flashlight. "Look, man. I'm sorry about that snake bullshit. I was just fucking with you. I wanted to get you all freaked out, then bring up the concept of death. It's all shamanic and shit. They would go through a symbolic death and be reborn as someone new. It's like part of shamanic warrior training. I thought that since it was your first time on shrooms, and we were out here in the desert, that you could have a true rebirth experience. Y'know, the kind of thing I wish I had my first time. A fucking let go of your life experience, something to crack your shell and let your spirit free. I guess I kind of screwed that one up."

I didn't buy it. This nice guy routine was just out of character for him. He was fucking patronizing me, and I was just not believing it. I struggled harder against the rock wall I climbed. He still was talking: "Dude, I am totally feeling them. I'm sorry I can't hold this flashlight still, but they make me shake. It's a super fantastic trip this time, even better than last time, so no wonder if was overwhelming. Damn. That guy always knows where to find the best shrooms."

I had finally reached the top. He offered his hand to me, but I refused it, pulling myself up by my own shaking muscles. Once out of the crevice, I crouched and caught my breath. All my muscles ached, and there was a searing pain in my leg.

"Look, I'm sorry man," he started to say, but trailed off when I turned my head away from him. He stood there awkwardly for a while, the shaking flashlight trained on me, but I ignored him, staring out into the dark desert and making my plans.

"I'm going to go back to the fire then," he said in a resigned, almost rebuffed voice. Another trick. He turned and began to walk back, the flashlight in front of him.

Adrenaline and hate rushed through my vein, as I turned toward him. This was my chance, probably my only chance. I collected the fragments of my will back together. As silent as I could, I took the knife out of the Velcro sheath. Though the sound was louder than I hoped, it didn't seem like he heard me.

It was now or never. I ran, just pushing towards him on my will alone, barely aware of my body or anything else. He kept shakily walking back to the fire, unaware of my assault. At the last second I think he may have heard me, but it was too late. I lunged forward and drove my knife into his back.

He screamed and stumbled. My own momentum and lack of coordination rammed me into him, tackling him to the ground. He began to twist and ask what was going on, but I ignored him. I knew what I had to do.

Using one hand, I held his damned snake head down on the ground by the back of his neck, so he couldn't bite me. I pulled the knife out of his back, then put it at the side of his neck. I think I heard the vague sound of his panicked "What are you doing?" before I yanked it across his arteries.

Pulling back, I crouched, the bloody knife ready for resistance that would never come. I stared at his form and the blood that gushed out of him, waiting for him to die.

When he was finally dead, I crashed as the adrenaline finally subsided. The hand that held the knife in a death grip suddenly unclenched. The bloody blade tumbled to the ground.

I found myself crying. Not just tears, but sobbing too. I didn't know what was going on, nothing made sense, and I kept crying. I had just killed someone, and there was no way I could wrap my head around it. He was trying to kill me and I had killed him in self defense. But it still made no sense to me. It was all too much.

For the next few minutes I paced back and forth across the ground, doing my best to stay out of his blood spatters, so my boots remained unstained. I didn't know what to do. I talked to myself as I paced. I needed a plan. Any plan. There was a dead body. I had to do something with that. The police might come. Would the police come? Would anyone find the body?

Some semblance of calm finally hit me. I couldn't tell the police. They wouldn't understand - how could they understand? Nobody could understand. That meant I had to get rid of the body. Nobody would care unless they found the body. This was the middle of nowhere, nobody would come searching here, I just had to make sure they didn't find it by accident. As long as the body was hidden...

I know what you're thinking. This was madness. Drug-addled madness. But you don't understand. Ted wanted to kill me. I think he wanted to kill me... But I was not going to go prison for him either way. So I needed to hide the body. I needed to hide what I had done.

I threw the body into crevice.

There, I said it.

I threw that body as deep down into that goddamn crevice as I could.

I'm not happy about that. But I don't think I regret it either.

After that, I cleaned myself up using clothes from his pack. I pushed his motorcycle down into the crevice with him, along with all his other possessions.

Then I got on my bike and rode as far away from there as I could. It may have been hours, it may have been minutes, I don't know. I rode until I couldn't ride anymore. Then I pulled off the road, took out my sleeping bag, and slept.

My dreams were full of blood and poison, the signposts on a journey through the dark bowels of the earth.

I rode aimlessly for the next few days, just trying to process the experience. What had really happened? We had both been on drugs, so I began to second guess everything that happened. I saw that the bite on my arm had been made with human teeth, not fangs. But that was a single detail, it didn't invalidate all my other fears. But what had been real and what had been delusion?

Every time I wonder if it was all confusion and insanity, I stop and wonder why he had brought me there. Why that spot? What about that crevice? Were there other bones there? If it was just an innocent trip, why did we end up at a killing place?

I finally returned home to Austin. I've tried to resume my life as best I could, but the weight is too much. Some days are okay, but on others, the gravity of it all and the lies I've had to tell threaten to break me. I didn't think I could hold this secret in any longer. The dreams are just...

When I was asked what happened to Ted at my job, I told them that he decided to stay in San Diego. I explained that he clearly said, "Fuck that job!" and that he found a girl in San Diego. I've been asked about him a few times by other people we both knew in common. Despite the lie, they always believe my explanation, because that's exactly how Ted was; it's easy to believe he'd just take off and leave his job behind. But even though they believe me, I'm nervous and shaking every time I answer. I'm worried that one of these times someone's going to notice.

I can't sleep at night. My dreams are full of snakes, blood, and that damn crack in the earth. Sometimes I wake up, only vaguely aware that I was just being told something by a giant snake, its words lost in the light of the morning. The only thing that remains is a feeling of dread and a dark hunger... one that can't be sated no matter how much I eat.

There's a great darkness that exists in the American Southwest, but I worry that the darkness isn't actually real, that it exists only for me. There's either some dark presence older than man whose hunger never ceases or the guilty stain of truth that I killed an innocent. I still don't know exactly what happened out there. That night seems just like a lost dream that has marred my consciousness and the only time it feels real and vivid is when I fall asleep...

That's why I need your help. I'm going insane not knowing. The dreams are driving me mad. They're pulling me apart and I need to know. I need someone to verify things. I need someone to tell me the truth.

I want you to come with me, out into the Southwest. We'll go to that same spot in New Mexico, turning at the snake fang tree and riding on to the dead tree campsite. We'll go to that crevice, that gaping maw in the earth, and I want you to look inside it. I need you to see the bodies. I need you to see if there are the bodies of dozens of dead men killed by a cult, or if there is only one body, a poor fool and its motorcycle.

I need to know the truth. The whispering in my dreams is growing so loud! I hear it in the daytime now when I lose focus and find myself daydreaming. It tells me I need to go out there, to find the truth... and that I need to bring a friend.

You've always been a good friend. You've now listened to my whole story and you know how insane it all sounds, but you know I'm not someone to make things up. Please, I need to know the truth.

Will you help me?

The Devil Takes His Cut

1

Dutch huffed as he climbed the wet rock outcropping. His old bones ached, the adrenaline that burned through his veins failing to offset the toll his life had taken on him. He was too old for this by too many years. They both were. His partner, Red, was following right behind him, his own complaints smothered by wheezing breath. Dutch had called Red "kid" for much of their friendship, but even his younger partner was getting on in years. They were too old for this game. They should have gotten out years ago. The outlaw game was for younger men with itching trigger fingers and a whole life ahead of them waiting to be cut short with a bad decision.

A shot ricocheted off a nearby rock, echoing through the rocks and fog. It pulled Dutch from his thoughts and redoubled his climbing efforts. The two outlaws had fled into the mountains to try to escape the mounted lawmen behind them. They hadn't been caught yet, but neither had they lost the lawmen. The trail unexpectedly led to a narrow pass, the mountain on one side of the trail and rocky outcroppings edging a drop into a ravine on the other side. If they had stayed on the trail the mounted lawmen would run them down, so they began climbing, trying to keep the rocks between them and the guns of the law.

Dutch couldn't tell if the weather was trying to help or hinder them. They began climbing as the sun was going down and then a fog rolled in, lowering visibility and making all the rocks slick. There was a thunderstorm coming too - Dutch already heard the far off rumble between gunshots.

They were being pursued by Marshal Thompson. A federal lawman who had never met an Indian he didn't want to kill, an officer of the peace who never left a town without orphaning some kid, Thompson's reputation was for always seeing the law to its final and fatal conclusion. He never made excuses and he never failed. Now he was after Dutch and Red, which meant that they would be hunted until dead. That was Thompson's code and the outlaws' death sentence.

Thompson had five other men with him. The younger, more reckless part of Dutch used to find that fair odds: six men, six rounds in his revolver. That younger man was now gone, along with the ammo in his pistol. Dutch didn't even have six rounds left in his revolver. He had been saving his shots, but he was still running out. Bullets weren't cheap. Every time he fired, Dutch could see the money that sped out of his barrel. Now that he was down to his last two rounds, he was wishing he had spent the money for just a few more before starting this job.

This all started over money, which was what it was always about. Dutch always thought it was stupid to risk your life over pride or respect. You either risk your life for money or to stay out of jail. Pride got men killed. Respect got men murdered. Only stupid men die for anything other than money and freedom.

Dutch had seen enough dead outlaws over the years. He had few friends left; too many died with a gut full of lead or at the end of a noose. Getting old as an outlaw meant seeing everyone he ever knew die as he counted the days until it was time for him to settle up with the reaper. Maybe that day would be today.

It was supposed to have been an easy job; low risk and easily pulled off even by two aging criminals like Dutch and Red. Hold up the courier and get the money that was within the saddlebags. Nobody knew the courier was carrying the money, which was the genius of both the bank who sent him and Dutch's holdup. No additional guards meant nobody would suspect the money; no additional guards meant two outlaws in the know would have an easy job.

Dutch should have known it would have gone wrong just from that. It's never an easy job.

The actual robbery had gone off well - the courier had cooperated and then kept his hands up. But then it all went to hell when Dutch heard the gallop of horses. Thompson and his lawmen were just passing by, but that lawman had the Devil's luck. As if he knew the outlaws were there, him and his men came riding around the bend. Within seconds their guns had been out and firing. Hoping he could end it quickly, Dutch had fired off a few shots. He had been sure his aim was dead on for Thompson, yet somehow the marshal rode on unscathed, not even concerned about the rounds coming his way, the men behind somehow taking the bullets meant for the marshal. Dutch rarely missed, so something strange had run through him at that moment, some fearful intuition. The two outlaws had barely made it onto their horses before the chase was on. They had managed to take the saddlebags of money with them but now they had six lawmen on their trail.

Dutch and Red's horses had died a mile back. Red had managed to grab his saddlebag full of loot, but the other had fallen under Dutch's horse. Their share of the loot had just been cut in half.

"The Devil take it!" spat Red as they fled from the dead horses. Dutch did a double take on his partner before running for the cover of the mountain pass.

And here they were not long after, climbing wet rocks in the fog, looking for escape as the lawmen's rifles sought their backs. The low visibility in the fog meant they could barely see the men shooting at them, just a muzzle flash in the fog. They were climbing rocks in the middle of nowhere looking for an escape they weren't even sure existed. As Dutch's arms and legs heaved on the climb, he began to regret.

As if answering the feeling inside him, the fog cleared like curtains parting. In the dying twilight lit by a rising full moon, there was something in the west, slouched on a ridge. For a moment, Red and Dutch looked in wonder. It was an old fort, the walls almost glittering from the moisture in the moonlight like some holy place. At first they worried that soldiers might assist the lawmen, but it became clear the fort was abandoned. No flag flew, no lamps glimmered, and the walls weren't manned. The fort squatted in a foreboding silence.

Red saw it as an opportunity. Even an old abandoned fort would give them refuge. If they closed the gate, even two men might defend it against six. The fort could even have extra ammunition or a tunnel out. Red saw it as real hope where they had none.

The fort meant something very different to Dutch. He had seen that fort before; he had been there decades ago. The fort had been in another place, many miles from here, yet this was unmistakably that same fort. How had their reckless escape led them back here? As a young man, Dutch had stood in that fort and he had made a deal. A horrible, infernal deal between one outlaw and a very different sort of outlaw. Dutch had gotten his part of the deal but the other hadn't taken his cut just yet.

Dutch reared back as if the fort was on fire, nearly losing his grasp on the rocks. He was not going back there. Nothing would ever take him back there. The memory of that fort might be burned into his memory, but he'd never set foot in it again as long as he lived if he had any say about it.

Red had other ideas. "Hot damn! That's our ticket!" he said, standing up on the rocks to move toward the fort. Instead of keeping low, he was now out of cover, an obvious figure silhouetted in front of the moon. Dutch saw this clearly and so did the lawmen.

It was at that moment that Dutch realized that Red was going to die. Seeing his partner in front of the moon, there was a certainty he knew in his bones. Red was doomed. This was Red's last ride. What was still uncertain was whether Dutch would go down with him.

"No, wait!" shouted Dutch, but it was too late.

At first Dutch couldn't tell if it was a gunshot or thunder, as the sky flashed with lightning at just that moment. But a second later he heard the roll of thunder and saw Red's body stiffen. Anything Red might have said was lost in the noise. Dutch watched in horror as his partner clutched at his gut and stumbled across the rocks. Red teetered on the edge, trying to keep his balance, one hand on his gut and the other on the saddlebag full of money. It was a strange sort of dance, Dutch holding his breath and wishing for Red's success. But then Red lost the battle. It took just an instant, but Red toppled off the rocks into the ravine.

Dutch stood still for just a moment, staring at the empty space where Red had just been, not believing it happened. But then as realization came rushing to him, he frantically pulled himself forward to try to look down into the ravine. As soon as Dutch moved, the air exploded with gunshots. He fired back twice, using his last bullets, the action causing the lawmen to pause their own shooting and take cover. In this brief respite, Dutch looked over the edge. He stared into the darkness, trying to see the bottom of the ravine, but his eyes strained to make out anything. The fog had begun rolling back in, so what visibility he had quickly disappeared.

A bullet glanced off the rock next to him. He was thankful the lawmen were terrible shots. Without thinking, Dutch jumped over the edge, using his boots against the side of the ravine to slow his descent. The side was sloped enough that he slid down most of the ravine in a cloud of dirt and kicked up gravel which covered his clothes and filled his lungs. But his luck was not to last. His boot hit a solid rock and twisted, causing him to tumble the last one hundred feet to the bottom.

He hit the bottom of the ravine where a shallow stream ran through it. He laid there for a minute, waiting for the pain to subside. He was sure he hadn't broken anything, but he was bruised and scraped up. He hurt, but he could keep running. That was all that mattered. An outlaw needs to be able to do two things: shoot and run. When he couldn't do one of those, it was time he was put down.

Dutch pulled himself to his feet, trying to get his bearings. He sat up, looking for Red. Dutch needed to find his partner. That was all that mattered. As he pulled his aching body to his feet, for just a moment the thought crossed his mind: which did he actually care about: Red or the money?

2

Dutch found Red laying in the shallow water, his blood washing away in the trickling stream. He wasn't face down, but he wasn't moving either.

"Red! Red!" said Dutch as he sloshed through the water to his partner.

Red had been shot in the gut. Dutch knew that a man could last for a few miserable days with a gut shot or be gone suddenly. Red wasn't answering and he wasn't moving, so maybe he had gone to the old shootout in the sky. Dutch saw that Red's hand still clutched the strap of the saddlebag. Red was gone, the money was better left with the living. Dutch grabbed the strap, giving it a slight tug.

Red let out a feeble groan.

"Red!" said Dutch. "Talk to me, you bastard!"

"They shot me, Dutch," wheezed Red.

"They sure did, Red," said Dutch. "And you fell down a goddamn mountain!"

"Is that why the rest of me hurts?" coughed Red with as much of a smile as he could muster. He coughed a few more times, that bare line of a smile disappearing from his face. "I'm hurt real bad, Dutch."

"Can you walk?"

"Damned if I know," Red whispered. "Need yer help to even stand."

Dutch nodded, leaning down to help his partner up. There was a part of Dutch who regretted going for the money so quickly; he should have confirmed Red was dead and that Dutch couldn't help. Red groaned a few times but didn't ask Dutch to stop. He finally got Red standing, the younger man clutching his gut and leaning on Dutch for support.

"It hurts like the Devil," said Red. "But I can walk."

Dutch tried to ignore his friend's turn of a phrase as they started to walk forward. They both knew that they couldn't stay where they were. The lawmen would figure out a way down into the ravine to see their corpses one way or another. Thompson never gave up. The two outlaws were moving slower now, but perhaps they could throw the lawmen off their trail. Dutch decided they should go downstream, though honestly he had no idea where they were. They walked in the stream, trying to hide their tracks within the water. There was no fog down in the ravine, so they could see well enough to pick their footing.

"If we get out of this, I'm givin' it all up," wheezed Red.

"Givin' what all up?" said Dutch.

"The outlaw life," said Red. "It's over for me. If this ain't the bullet to end me, the next one will be. Even I know those are bad odds."

Dutch said nothing. He had some of the same thoughts. The world was changing - there was no room for outlaws anymore. It was too easy for lawmen. Dutch knew his and Red's wanted posters were hanging in nearly every sheriff's office. *Wanted: Dead or Alive*. They were having a hard time going anywhere; they were starting to be recognized in towns they had never been to before. The game was getting harder and harder each year. And nobody else was playing. Their friends were all dead. They might as well be the last outlaws.

Of course, maybe it wasn't the world that was changing, maybe it was them. Each year they got older. Their reflexes got more sluggish, their sight got a little fuzzier, their aim got a little worse, their run got a little slower. Maybe they were just two old men that couldn't be worthwhile outlaws anymore. They were two has-beens holding out as long as they could against an inevitability. They had fought a good war in their lives, but that war was going to kill them if they didn't leave it to younger men.

They walked for what felt like an hour, Red's blood dripping into the stream. They were walking downstream, so instead of leaving a trail, they got to see Red's life rush away as soon as it dripped. Then the rain came. It was a cold rain that chilled them to the bone. Red felt twice as heavy when soaking wet and the storm made Dutch's joints ache even more. He knew they needed to find some place to hole up until the storm passed, if not the whole night.

Dutch thought the fog was rolling in ahead of them, but he realized it wasn't fog when he smelled it. It was a thick smoke that smelled like a strange tobacco. It was familiar, but he couldn't place it.

"Chang's opium den?" said Red lazily. Dutch looked at him and wondered if he was delirious.

The smoke was coming out of a cave tucked into the side of the ravine. Dutch knew that tobacco meant there was someone inside, but he didn't know who. Indians? Thompson and his men? He didn't fancy getting shot down as soon as he walked through that smoke, but they needed to get out of the rain and warm up by a fire. Red was definitely going to die if they didn't find somewhere to rest soon.

Pulling Red with him, Dutch stepped down into the cave entrance, glad for a moment to be out of the rain. The sweet smelling smoke filled the opening and Dutch couldn't see farther in.

"Hello?" said Dutch hesitantly.

"Come inside, friend," said an accented voice from within.

Dutch knew it at least wasn't Marshal Thompson, so he decided to take his chances. Walking forward, he was momentarily blinded by the smoke. While it pleased his nose, it made his eyes sting. It was another moment before he blinked away tears and his red eyes scanned the interior of the cave.

The cave was lit by a flickering fire in the center of the room. The fire was burning in a circle of large stones with a black grate over it. Clearly this fireplace had been built long ago. The ceiling was low, just above Dutch's head. The room was filled with strange colored silks, Persian rugs, and rattan boxes. Next to the fire was a strange man. His skin was dark, but not like an ex slave. He was thin and wore no shirt. He had a grand beard of dark, wiry hair and wore a strange hat of green silk decorated with gold. He sat cross-legged, not like an Indian, but weirdly straight, like some Oriental Dutch had seen on a trip out to the coast. The man's face was the strangest part. Almost a caricature of a person, he had a long nose, a pronounced brow, and sharp cheek bones. His eyes were unfathomable, shadowed in the recesses below his brow. He held the pipe of a hookah at the corner of his mouth, his head cocked in a vaguely amused expression. The tube for the pipe led off into a pile of silks, the rest of the hookah seemingly hidden.

Dutch could swear this man was familiar, but he could never recall meeting a man like this.

"Come," said the man, unmoving. "Put him down and rest, friend." Removing the pipe, he gestured to two pallets of multicolored silk on top of rugs.

Dutch nodded and gently laid Red down on one of the pallets. He adjusted Red so that he would be comfortable but also not bleed so much on the silk. Dutch noticed that the smoking man sat on his own pallet, so there had been two empty pallets in front of him before Dutch and Red had entered.

"My friend is hurt," said Dutch. "We need rest, but I need to get him to a doc."

The man stared at Dutch, the hookah pipe between his lips, seemingly motionless. Then he opened his mouth and smoke spilled out... and kept spilling out. A seemingly endless stream of smoke billowed out of the man's mouth, far more than lungs could hold, especially for a man who gave no sign of exertion. The smoke smelled of tobacco and rose petals.

"I am no doctor," said the accented voice after finishing his exhale. "Nor are there any nearby that can help him. But please, partake of my supplies if you wish." He gestured vaguely to particular a rattan box.

Dutch looked at the man strangely but said nothing. He grabbed the box and opened it. He found bandages, a needle and thread, and a bottle of something he couldn't determine. Not knowing what he was doing, he only grabbed the bandages. Dutch was no doctor and never had the stomach to watch as Doc Churchill fiddled around with a man's innards, so he paused for a moment before figuring out just how to bandage Red. He settled for awkwardly wrapping the man's abdomen - over his clothes. He positioned Red's hand to hold down on the wound.

"I got a stomach ache, Ma," said Red vaguely. Dutch noticed sweat on the man's brow. Fever delirium.

Dutch sat back down on his pallet, knowing Red might not last out the night.

"Thank you for yer hospitality," said Dutch.

"There is a time for hospitality," said the man's accent, his voice lengthening some words in an almost Oriental slur, "and there is a time for bargains. Just as there is a time to sow and there is a time to reap. All things in their time."

"I can't say I understand," said Dutch, trying to probe the shadows that hid the smoking man's eyes.

The man nodded, suddenly interested in looking at something off to the side. "I am a merchant of a kind, yes? I deal in... let's say difficult to find items. It occurs to me that safety, like hospitality, is invaluable in the right circumstances. Is it not?" said the man, turning back to look at Dutch.

Dutch's hand involuntarily went to his revolver. He remembered it was empty, but this man didn't know that.

"Not from me," said the man, understanding Dutch's movement. "But you are hiding. Outlaws, are you not?"

Dutch's hand tensed at his revolver. "What if we are?"

The man opened his mouth to let out another enormous belch of billowing smoke. This time it smelled of tobacco and cinnamon. "I can keep you safe from those that are chasing you." He paused meaningfully. "For a price."

Dutch suddenly wondered how this man would know someone was after them. But then he remembered the gunshots. They had echoed through the mountains. Of course this little man in his cave had heard them. Dutch would have surprised if he hadn't.

"Yer sayin' you could guarantee our safety?" said Dutch.

"For a price."

Dutch was dubious of whether this thin man would be able to guarantee anything, but he also knew that Red and him needed to hide out somewhere. And this little cave would fit the bill nicely. If this man was a merchant, as he said, perhaps he had a wagon somewhere that would sneak them out of the mountains.

"And jus' what price is that?" asked Dutch.

The man did not answer, but his gazed turned and he nodded toward Red. Dutch looked over and saw the saddlebag still resting on Red's shoulder, filled with money. Again, Dutch wondered how this man knew, but remembered the man was shrewd. Two half dead outlaws stumble in our of the rain, holding tightly to one saddlebag despite a gut shot. Of course the bag had something valuable. He simultaneously gained respect and disgust for the man.

When Dutch didn't respond, the man spoke. "You are always free to take your chances."

Dutch looked toward the opening of the cave where the smoke was billowing out into the night. He didn't want to leave. He didn't want to risk both their lives in the rain with Thompson's men out there. He also knew this man had him over a barrel. Without ammo in his revolver, overpowering him was going to be risky. This man might have a pistol hidden among the silk. No, that wasn't an option. It all came down to just a simple question. What were their lives worth?

"Fine, you win," said Dutch.

"Eh?" said the man, cocking his head.

"I agree," said Dutch. "We need to be safe. I'll pay yer godddamn fee. It jus' better be worth it."

"I am a merchant - "

"*Of a sort*, you said," interrupted Dutch.

"Yes, of a sort, but I am good to my word. A bargain is a bargain."

Dutch nodded, not altogether happy with the deal. But it was done. He laid back on the pallet, trying to at least enjoy the comfort and safety he had just bought. A few minutes passed and Dutch began to feel drowsy, but the strange man's words brought him back to alertness.

"Your friend has died."

There was no urgency, no emotion to the statement. It was a flat statement of fact. The man was calmly sitting with his pipe, his back as straight as ever.

Dutch sat back up and then crawled over to Red. The younger man's hand had fallen away from the bandages, which were stained red with blood. Dutch put his hand near Red's nose and felt for breath. There was none.

Something like sadness gripped Dutch's heart. He would have said he was too old, too hardened for sadness. He had seen more than enough loss and had buried partners before. But this he felt. Maybe because it was coiled up with the regret in his heart. He would have cried if that part of him hadn't shriveled up and died long ago. He simply reached into his pocket and took his last two coins. He laid them on Red's eyes. Payment for the afterlife.

Dutch crawled back onto his own pallet, grabbing a multicolored blanket to wrap around him.

"All things end," said the smoking man, his eyes still lost in shadows.

The old outlaw said nothing, but stared at the man, trying to pierce the shadows of his eyes. The strange man opened his mouth again and smoke endlessly billowed out again. This time it smelled foul, reminiscent of the time Dutch had crawled through a mine for a bag of a dead man's gold. And unlike the other times the man had breathed out smoke, it kept flowing out the man's open mouth for an impossibly long time. This foul smoke filled the entire room until Dutch couldn't see anything.

Dutch would have stood up, he would have panicked, but for some reason the smoke was strangely calming. Instead of afraid, he felt drowsy. In fact, all cares seemed to float away as he found himself drifting into an almost pleasant unconsciousness. The voice of danger in the back of his head screamed in futility until Dutch was out.

3

It was morning when Dutch awoke, a weak crack of daylight spilling in where the cave opening and the ravine aligned just right. The smoke from the night before was gone, leaving just a lingering sulfurous smell. As he sat up, Dutch realized the smoke wasn't the only thing missing. So were the silk, the rugs, the rattan containers, the hookah, and especially the strange smoking man.

The burned out fire still had its black grate on top of old stones, but gone were all traces of the merchant-of-a-sort. In fact, somehow the pallet Dutch had slept on was missing as well.

When he looked over for Red's body, that too was gone. Dutch crawled over to look at the spot where his partner laid, finding no trace of even blood. In Red's place were just a few items that made Dutch's own blood run cold. The saddlebag was still there, and he confirmed all the money was still in it. Next to it was a bloodstained gun belt. This wasn't Red's belt nor was it Dutch's. This had bullet pockets stretched across it bandolier-style, and every pocket was filled with a round. The last two items almost went unnoticed, but once Dutch saw them, he could never forget them.

Exactly where Red had laid were the two coins Dutch had placed over his eyes.

Dutch grabbed the belt and strapped it on, trying to not even think about all the questions he had. He numbly put six rounds in his revolver and slid it into the pocket of the new belt. It fit perfectly. He grabbed the saddlebag and threw it over his shoulder. He did not touch the coins.

As he stepped out of the cave, it was as if some weight was pulled off him. There was something heavy in that cave, even without the strange man occupying it. As he stepped away from it, he could almost feel it pressing behind him, as if invisible smoke still billowed out of the cave. Why had Red and he come there? And where had Red gone?

He was startled from his reverie by the neigh of a horse. He looked over to see a group of mounted Indians dressed for war. He saw the war paint on their faces, scalps at their belt, and the rifles over their shoulders. He expected to see violence etched in their features, ready to kill him. But their faces weren't angry, just bewildered as they looked at him. One Indian was embarrassed, struggling to control the horse that had neighed.

Dutch stood still. He had the loaded revolver at his belt. As a younger man, he could have taken all these Indians without worry. But he was now an older man, slower and still shaken by his experiences in the cave. He'd fight if he had to, but if he could talk his way out, he would. Some part of him was amused that after all his running from Thompson, he might die by Indians that Thompson would gladly kill.

The Indians just stared at Dutch, their obvious leader in thought, the other men uneasy. All their horses were nervous, not just the one which was now under control.

When none had said anything, Dutch finally asked, "Do y'all speak English?"

"We were wondering if *you* did," said the leader. "Are you even a man?"

Dutch looked down at himself and stretched out his left arm, as if giving the Indians a better look. His right arm never strayed far from his revolver. He stared back at the Indians in confusion. "You got eyes, dontcha?"

"You look like a white man," said the leader thoughtfully. "But maybe you only have the form of one. If you come out of that place, maybe you are not a man at all." He pointed at the cave.

Dutch turned back and looked at the cave. In the light of day, it looked less impressive. The opening was more just a crack in the rock, as if split by a bolt of thunder. Nothing remained of the scented smokes or merchant of the evening before.

"The cave?" said Dutch. "I hid out from the storm there. What's so special about the damn cave?"

"Storm?" The leader shared a look with one of his men before turning back to Dutch. "The cave is special. It is both a cave but not a cave. It's more than a cave and less than a place. We don't go inside; it is forbidden. It is a bad place. Those that come out of the cave are not men. What are you?"

Dutch looked back at the cave again. It all fell into place. The cave, the fort, the man with his hookah. The same as before. Last time Dutch had met him, he had been a disgraced army colonel, but it was him. And Dutch had made a deal again. That was why Red was gone.

He wanted to scream. He wanted to cry. He wanted to shout out in anger. But ultimately, he just laughed. It was madness. The only appropriate response was laughter.

"I reckon I ain't sure if I am a man anymore," said Dutch with bitter amusement. "I guess you could say I am jus' a prisoner of the past, a soldier of a dying way. A fool who keeps makin' the same mistakes. I've sold everything that mattered to watch all my friends die. I reckon that I jus' wear the skin of a white man 'cause it still suits me to."

It was a flippant response, half a joke, but it represented the cracked way Dutch felt. It was all a big joke. It hadn't been a deal, it was goddamn theater. That man had always been playing with Dutch, watching him dance as he pulled the strings, but the outlaw's part was not over yet. He laughed again, keeping his hand loose to draw his gun. Some reflexes never die.

Despite the laughter and joke, the Indians didn't attack. Instead the leader stared at Dutch for a moment. Then he nodded.

"If you were a white man, we would kill you and take your scalp," said the leader. "But you are no white man, so we walk away. No quarrel with you, He Who Walks Like a Man."

"Why are you killin' white men? This ain't your territory, is it?"

The leader shook his head. "It is not. But white men raped one of the daughters of our tribe. Now we make war and scalp all white men until we are satisfied." He paused and looked to his men before his voice turned icy. "And we are not yet satisfied."

"Seems to me, satisfaction is a hard thing to come by," said Dutch, "particularly for men of violence."

The leader nodded while his Scalphunters all grinned. "That is true. But that knowledge does nothing for our anger. So we'll collect a few more scalps."

Dutch nodded too. "I'll tell you what. I jus' happen to know a few white men around here who are worth killin'."

"Are you so quick to turn on your brothers?" asked the leader.

"You forget," said Dutch with a grin, "I am no man. They ain't my brothers."

The leader nodded. "You speak the truth."

"And how about this?" said Dutch. "What if I face these white men with you?"

The leader and his men looked at Dutch for a long moment. Then the leader laughed. Then the other Scalphunters laughed. And so did Dutch.

* * *

High on the ridge, Dutch wasn't sure if Thompson and his men could see him and the Scalphunters. The outlaw and his allies were mounted on horses, but the setting sun was at their back. Thompson's posse was setting up a camp. They had been chasing two old outlaws, so they didn't expect an assault. They were the hunters, not the hunted. And that was their mistake.

Dutch thought of the ridiculousness of it all. Outlaw or soldier, criminal or law man, anyone who straps on a gun is heading for the same fate. Blood leads to blood. The first time they held a gun, they made a deal with the Devil. They pulled the trigger and signed on the dotted line. And the Devil always takes his cut.

Looking down from the ridge with the light of the setting sun, Dutch examined Thompson and his men. They were old too. Not a young man among them. It was the sad fact: young men weren't picking up the gun. It was an old man's game. As the world changed, all of them gathered here would be outlaws, outsiders in a world that had moved past them. The world of the heroes of the gun was dying and they were all hurrying themselves to their deaths.

He turned and looked at the Scalphunters next to him. They knew it as well. Their world was ending too. Their war was a dying gasp before it was all over. They had also decided to trade a slow death for a feverish blaze of vengeance.

It was true what Dutch had told the Scalphunters. He didn't know if he was a man anymore. All he knew was that he was an outlaw and he knew that would never be over. As he pulled his revolver from his holster, he realized his true calling. "War is my trade, killing is all that I have ever been good at."

"Second thoughts, He Who Walks Like a Man?" said the leader of the Scalphunters.

With a mirthless grin, Dutch shook his head. He cocked the hammer on his revolver and signaled the Scalphunters. All around him, the Scalphunters spurred their horses into motion, screaming a war cry. Dutch rode with them, but he stayed silent. His war cry came out the barrel of his gun.

Thompson's men broke into a panic, seeing a group of raging Indians riding down upon them, guns firing. The posse began shooting and shouting too. It was chaos, old men falling to the ground in a spray of blood and gunpowder. Thompson himself kept his cool. With confidence, he simply drew his gun and aimed, taking all the time in the world before firing. He didn't fear death. He knew he had the Devil's luck.

Dutch caught Thompson's eye and the two stared at each other. Something ran between them. They both knew. They both had the same regret, the same advantage. Now it was time to see who had made the better deal.

Even as Dutch rode forward, his revolver delivering death to men who had stalked him, driving his horse toward Thompson for an inevitable duel, he realized it didn't matter. None of it mattered. In some forgotten corner of the world, they fought their war, the last outlaws seeking their deaths, but none of it really mattered. Live or die today, they were all fools.

Because in the end, no matter the winner or loser, no matter who was right and who was wrong, no matter which corpses who lay on the ground and which walked away, the Devil always takes his cut.

Balls

Inevitably, conversation turned to my balls. It's rare that I have any sort of conversation at all these days without the other person maneuvering it to the subject of my balls. I'm just used to its inevitability like I am the eventual heat death of the universe.

"Do they require a lot of maintenance for your job?" she asked. "Your balls, I mean."

"There's some required," I said, having been through these questions many times before.

"Like, do you spend hours in the bathroom shaving them, making sure every contour is right?" she pressed. "Or do you use some liquid hair removal solution? And do you like, go somewhere for that? A spa?"

"It doesn't matter," I said tiredly. I enjoyed the attention and my balls are one of my preferred subjects, but I get the same questions over and over. "Since I wear briefs, the status of my pubes doesn't matter unless it's sticking out of the briefs."

She looks impressed, so I guess that was the answer she was looking for.

I guess you're wondering why I always get those questions and why I sometimes tire of attractive women asking about my nether regions. It's not as sordid as you think.

You see, I'm a male underwear model.

Imagine, if you will, that you're flipping through the latest department store catalog, looking to see the season's best from Macy's or LL Bean. Maybe you're just looking for a comfortable sweater that's appropriate for the season. As you flip through the catalog searching for the perfect turtleneck, you happen upon the male underwear section. It is there that you see a series of men - secular avatars of Adonis - posed and strutting in masculine postures, their hips thrust out, their arms akimbo, dressed only in the eternal question of boxers or briefs. Though they are attractive males tending towards either the beefcake or GQ conventions that show vast amounts of skin, they have been positioned in such a way that their near nakedness is not overtly sexual. It is only suggestive of male power and sexuality without the bending and twisting you see more often in female lingerie models.

Amongst such men you would find me, fists placed at my waist, back slightly arched, hips thrust forward, the bulge of my briefs thrust outward, the balls inside barely contained in their furious desire to dominate the world. That is my signature pose.

I have other poses, of course – in my line of work, I do not want to be inflexible with my expertise. But my signature pose is my power pose, the one where the true power of my balls shines, like a golden aura. If the photographer at a shoot has any sense, he'll pick my power pose and set me center stage - I am wasted as a back up to others. My balls shine best when they are the sun, the other models' hardware satellite to my own. But I can't always control the whims of the photographers, and so I must make do with second fiddle on occasion.

Also, briefs only. That's my rule. I only do briefs. I have my agent write it in all my contracts so that it is legal and unbreakable. They can't make me do boxers. I once walked off the set when some clearly amateur photographer tried to have me wear boxers. Even when I cited my contract, he just laughed. So when I walked off the set and left them in a lurch, they learned. It took some apologies and sweet talking from his assistant who came bearing gifts of single malt scotch and Red Vines to get me back on the set for the shoot. Even then, I deigned only to go as far as boxer briefs.

This is also a good time to dispel any lingering misconceptions about my career that may have surfaced. For once and for all, I am not a butt model. Never have been, never will be. In no catalog, ad, photo spread, or professionally done shoot will you see me turned around to show off my posterior. I'm not saying that my aft section is without its merits, it's simply not the strength I have chosen to market. You will never know me by my ass. My true marketability is in my crotch and I make that clear to any prospective photographer. If I am going to be photographed, it will be in briefs, my bulge fully exposed to the world and God.

Now let's talk about bulges, since we're on the subject. It is important to realize that absolutely no erections are involved in male underwear modeling. If you get hard, they have to pause the shoot and everyone has to wait around until *you* get your junk under control again. Male underwear photography is an erection free zone. Any picture of male underwear in a catalog must remain as inoffensive and non-threatening as possible. Any appearance or impression of the male wang should be as common and verifiable as a Loch Ness Monster sighting.

However, this brings us to the flip side. Clothing manufacturers are trying to get the underwear sold with those pictures. The audience for buying them is mostly men, but also their wives, their girlfriends, and assorted significant others. While the near-naked man must look non threatening, they cannot look androgynous, or the most unthinkable or all unthinkables: unmanly. As underwear models, we are to be paragons of the Platonic ideals of manhood, oiled up and poured into a marketable pair of underwear for mass consumption. Thus, while erections must be avoided, there needs to be some impression of male genitalia, some viewable outward expression of the divine grandeur of the Y chromosome. As the erection is taboo, the physicality of manhood in male underwear comes down to one thing, one primal feature, given to us by God and celebrated by culture.

Balls.

I'm always the first to point out that not enough academic attention has been given to balls across the ages. Sure, many scholars are quick to point out phallic representations in cultures, but few scholars give credits to the age-old depictions of cojones in world cultures. For example, did you know that the Mayans had a festival every year at the Summer Solstice honoring balls to give favor and virility to their warriors? They used hanging censors of incense to represent the pendulous nature of the Mayan warrior sack. Are the Mayans too obscure? Then let's talk something more European. Cultural anthropologists often gloss over the fact that the spherical ornaments we hang upon Christmas trees have a different origin. Like many other traditions co-opted into Christianity, these ornaments derive from age-old Black Forest rites that celebrate male virility and practiced on Walpurgisnacht. When you hang a glossy bulb on your Yuletide tree, you're honoring masculinity and the Jungian form of the ball sack.

This brings me to my secondary career, and how I met the young lady I spoke of at the outset of this story. Due to the lack of knowledge about the historical context of balls, something I found true even in academia, I spent years in study and research to gain advanced degrees in the subject. While officially my degrees were in Anthropology, I personally prefer to think of it as Cojonology or Male Gonadal studies. After years of research and publishing, I became an expert in the cultural context of balls. I met the young lady in my gig as traveling lecturer and Adjunct Professor of Gonadal Studies at Columbia University.

I was lecturing at another university on a Thursday at 8pm. The topic was "The Emergence of Balls within American Culture in the New Millennium." I was happy to find flyers up for the lecture around campus. Sometimes the social climates at universities are not as welcoming to my field of study as they could be. This university seemed to be more welcoming than most.

I make no secret of my other life as a male underwear model when I lecture. In fact, I believe it gives me a unique and personal perspective on the topic. In academia, many lecturers and professors are mere observers, removed from the cultural trends they are studying. They are on the outside looking in, which may cause them to miss details or the significance of certain things. I have no such problem. I am an actor and influencer in my own cultural trend, and I think that unique perspective is appreciated by my audience. Academia could use more "gonzo scholarship" where the scholar directly experiences their subject. However, I don't let my experience overwhelm my research, lest I tarnish or compromise my reputation or message.

It was because I used the context of my modeling career that I was approached after my lecture by the young lady I've referenced, Sally Monroe. She complimented my work in the Sears catalog of '13, which was a spread I was quite proud of. The merchandise was not quite Calvin Klein, but I really felt I showed it off well. They allowed me my signature pose, and I think I sold quite a large amount of pairs of underwear for the Sears Corporation. After such a compliment, I invited Sally out to have a drink and answer any questions she might have.

Over drinks I found that she claimed that she was a Women's Studies grad student at the university, but something was off, though I couldn't put a finger on it at the time. I also thought it curious that a Women's Studies major would have such an interest in my own research. She explained that though her focus was on the other type of genitalia, she understood the reason for my studies and had to admit she was intrigued. This part was not strange to me, as I had heard that sentiment before from other young co-eds and knew it was a new wave of awakening ball-awareness that was slowly making its way across America.

Despite a feeling that something was off, conversation was still quite pleasant as it wandered from topic to topic, whether related to the lecture or not (Her: "Did you know that in some parts of the world they actually eat the balls of animals? They believe they gain their virility." Me: "I had heard such a thing, but hope they don't move onto humans!") But inevitably, for all the academic talk and amusement, the topic of conversation drifted to my own, personal set of balls. She asked the tiresome question at the beginning of this story, but she continued in that direction.

"Tell me more about being an underwear model," she asked, coquettishly flipping her hair back. "Actually, tell me more about your balls," she said with a sly smile.

"I'm not sure what to say," I feigned, "What would you like to know about them?" I've been through this song and dance before. I've found hard-to-get works best.

"I know you're not really so modest," she said, "but I'll play along. I expect yours are bigger than average, allowing you to be, shall we say, ballsy? How do you compare to the other models?"

"I'd say I can hold my own among the best of them. But it's not for me to toot my own horn."

"Oh no, of course not," she said with a smile, "maybe I'd like to toot it." She's quicker than most.

"I'm sure that can be arranged," I replied. At this point she had been obvious, so why not stay on that level?

"Then arrange it already, and let's get out of here!" she said, laughing.

I'll admit here that this is not the first time I have been taken home by an attractive young lady. I make no excuses for it, and for all this talk about balls, I'm glad to have an opportunity to mention in passing my affection for parts of the female anatomy. This time, however, I don't mention my conquest merely to boast. What followed is its own story.

She took me back to the house she claimed she shared with another girl from the university. I say claimed, because in retrospect I wonder how much was true. She was younger than me, but she could have easily been older than college aged and simply dressing younger to mislead. I admit that I was thinking with a lower part of my anatomy at this point, so my thinking ignored a few inconsistencies.

Her roommate was conveniently out. We shared another drink in her living room, and while I flirted, her seduction was on maximum. So I'll make a long story short: we adjourned to her bedroom where we made the beast with two backs until we were satisfied. Afterward we laid back and partially disengaged before engaging in the complimentary snuggling. I was feeling rather spent, but I admit I enjoyed feeling her chest rise and fall in my arms.

Feeling lighthearted, I looked her in the eyes and said, "Well, Sally Monroe, how was your evening?"

She smiled, then got a funny look on her face that I couldn't discern. "Oh, it's not over yet."

I felt her disengage herself from me, and turned to reach towards her night table. The motion was very natural, and I remember thinking that she was just grabbing for a cigarette, a joint, or something like that. But at the same time, on the level of instinct, I knew something was wrong. I'm not sure how, but I rolled off the bed just as she swung her arm around, stabbing a knife into the place in the bed I had just vacated.

Holy crap! For all the casual sex I had in my life, this was the first time attempted murder was part of the post-coital activities. She seemed pleased with the sex, and if she hadn't actually been, stabbing is still *not* the way to criticize my sexual prowess. I suddenly wondered if she was one of those black widows that movies seemed to think actually existed. Was I the first? Or was the bed built on the bones of all her previous fucks?

I scrambled to my feet in the tangle of bed sheets on the side of the bed. She had pulled back into a fighting crouch. She leapt up, using the middle of the bed as a springboard to send her lunging at me. I dodged to the side and she sunk the blade into the wall instead of me.

We both scrambled for balance, me rising to my feet, and her to a crouch. She lunged at me, sinking the blade partly into the wall as I dodged to my right.

"What the fuck are you doing?" I shouted as I ran a few paces from her, vaguely holding onto a sheet that poorly covered my nakedness. I figured there should be some explanation forthcoming for the sudden knife skills she was showing me. I thought crazy people liked going on long monologues? No, wait, that was supervillains.

With a frenzied grunt, she pulled the knife out of the wall. I could see that it was not a kitchen knife. It looked decorated, like it was ceremonial or historical. I glinted silver in the low light. Of course, none of that was as important as the wicked-looking edge on that blade. She had a crazed look in her eyes as she turned towards me.

"I must have your power," she said. "And this is the time. Your balls are now empty. You've lost your power."

I backed against her dresser, moving along it to my right, to get more distance from her.

"That's not how it works!" I said. "Sure, it might be an hour or two before we can fuck again, but I assure you I am still quite powerful."

I'm not quite sure which power she was wondering about, but I figured I'd like. Outside of the power to gain an erection, I still felt quite strong. Maybe I needed to have a sports drink for what I sweated out, but I hardly felt my strength sapped by the Kryptonite of orgasm.

She started advancing on me, and I realized this wasn't the best approach at talking her out of her murderous act. One does not simply reason with crazy. Without my own knife I couldn't intimidate her, and it seemed that outright arguing with a crazy person was a recipe for stabbing. Maybe I could stall.

"What are you planning to do with that knife?" I asked, my eyes fixed on her knife that was in the air, the point seemed locked on my chest. I'm pretty sure I knew what she was going to do immediately, but I figured if I got her talking, I might come up with some idea. I darted my eyes left and right, looking for something to help me in the unfamiliar bedroom. To my right was a door, probably to her bathroom.

She laughed. "I'm going to cut your balls off," she said, "with this knife. What did you think I was going to do with it?"

Okay, so it wasn't *just* about death and stabbing. There was a method to her madness.

"What? Why?" I said. She hadn't moved forward, so I think I gained a moment by asking her to explain.

"I need their power for my ritual," she said. "Do you know the power you hold in your ball sack? Not only the power to help create life, but as a male model, you have the power to inspire others. Do you realize the fetish that could be created from your balls?"

I'm pretty sure she didn't mean the type of fetish I immediately thought of.

I'm sure I could have learned more about her strange logic. She probably *was* one of the crazy types that would talk and talk. But the subject matter was quickly becoming uncomfortable. It didn't matter if she wanted to sauté and eat my balls or use them to summon demons for world domination, the general idea of removing them from me was an uncomfortable subject. I really didn't want to know more about it. I already felt like my balls were shriveling up to try and hide in my body cavity. I had heard that Chinese martial artists had that ability and began wishing I had studied kungfu.

It was time for a quick and reckless decision. I charged the door to my right, bursting into a small bathroom. I slammed the door shut behind me and held my weight on it. I began fiddling with the handle, desperately trying to figure out how it locked in the dim light. The door shuddered against my weight and pushed open an inch as I felt her ram against it. I pushed harder and the door closed shut. I finally found the locking mechanism and twisted it with a click.

I stepped back, ready to put my weight back on the door if the lock didn't hold. A second later I saw her ram the door again. It shuddered, but it held... for now.

As I looked around the room, I was treated with a litany of insults as she banged on the door. She made sure to let me know that there was no escape, that she'd surely get me, and that I should open the fucking door. She also spent a lot of shouting to tell me what she was going to do to my balls once she got them. I'd rather not repeat any of that.

This bathroom was small, at best three feet wide by five feet long. She didn't clean her sink often enough, so it was covered with grime, hair, and nearly empty bottles of hair products. There was some serious grout in the shower. Clearly there was no crazy ritual for bathroom cleanliness.

I was still mostly naked, so when I saw a bathrobe hung up, I grabbed it and put it on. It was pink and frilly, but better than being naked. It was a little short on me, so my big legs stuck prominently out from under it. At least my balls were concealed.

There was a small window with frosted glass on one end of the bathroom above the toilet. It was kind of small, but large enough that I think I could push myself through it. I'm typically not so adventurous that I'd slide through second floor bathroom windows, but with a crazy woman with a knife banging on a fragile door, I was running out of options. I could try and fight, but no amount of towels or shampoo bottles seemed the equal of a sharp knife. So my best bet seemed the window. I hoped it didn't have any bars on the other side.

I opened the window and let out a loud creak, enough that she could hear it.

"What are you doing?" she said. There was some worry in that voice.

Cold air rushed in through the window, momentarily lifting the short skirt of my frilly pink bathrobe. I admit it caused some shrinkage. I looked out of the window and noticed it wasn't a direct drop. This window opened up onto the shingled roof. I wasn't sure what I was going to do on the roof, but it seemed way better than where I was.

As I climbed up on the toilet and started to wriggle my way out, I heard her voice change.

"Umm, so I think I need to apologize." Her voice was now surprisingly calm, if not a little bit whiny. It surprised me, but not enough to make me stop what I was doing. I didn't answer other than to grunt as I tried to slide my masculine frame through this window. I thought I could fit, but I often thought certain furniture would fit into my car when I bought it, and that often turned out to be wrong. I was severely fucked if I got stuck halfway through the window. It would be handing my balls to her on a silver platter... well, a pink frilly platter.

She continued without my response. "I'm sorry about that... about all this. I'm not sure what was going on with me, but I'm okay now. I haven't been taking my medication, because it's been making me feel strange. But it looks like I'm even stranger not on it. Won't you come out? We can talk about this back in the bedroom..."

I laughed to myself. It didn't matter whether she had a psychotic break or not, or if she was normal and nonviolent now (which I did not believe). The risk was too high and I was pretty sure that this was just a trick. I just wasn't going back there.

"We had such a good time earlier," she said. Her voice was calm and patronizing, but there was something else in her voice. Something desperate. I think she was afraid of my escape. "Maybe if it's been long enough, we can have some fun in bed again..."

Try it again so that you can castrate me with your ritual knife? Nice try, psycho girl.

Luckily, I didn't get stuck in the window and was able to pull myself out onto the roof. It was a cold and windy night, causing me to shiver. The roof shingles were rough under my bare feet. The wind was bad enough, but I was not dressed for it: I was wearing only a too-small pink frilly bathrobe, and more than just the robe was flapping in the wind.

I walked along the roof, my arms folded for warmth, and I gauged my options for escape. No matter which side of the roof, it looked like a thirty foot drop to the ground. The softest landing looked to be grass or bushes. Thirty feet looked particularly intimidating when looking down and thinking about jumping, particularly when you're thinking about making the jump half naked.

Then again, my other option was to climb back in the window and deal with Crazy McKnifeypants, which didn't seem like an option at all. This was confirmed when I starting hearing her ramming the door again. She grunted crazily each time she collided with it.

The bushes I could jump into seemed like a bad idea. I was in just a bathrobe and it looked like the bushes might be stinging nettles. Without ever having directly experienced it, I was pretty sure that stinging nettles would not mix with balls very well. The problem was, the bushes were really my only option.

The roof wasn't near another house. It was late at night on a cold night, so there were no pedestrians. I didn't have anything to flag someone down with and my phone was unfortunately in my pants back in the bedroom on the other side of a knife-wielding crazy person. I had no idea how long the bathroom door would hold, and I wouldn't put it past her to climb out here and resume her previous stabbing behavior.

I looked down at the bushes. They were still my top option. My time for decisions came to a close as I heard her break through the bathroom door with a crash and a triumphant scream. She'd be on the roof soon.

I took a deep breath. This was not the time for cowardice. My options were before me and it was time to step up and pick one, not pussy out. Like many other philosophers of masculinity, I had always stated that life should be lived courageously, balls out and brave. While I had tended to mean that metaphorically, that maxim was catching up to me with a very concrete situation. It was time to put my money where my mouth was and to put my courage into practice. Balls out.

Without fanfare, reservations, or even a flamboyant "Tally-ho!", I jumped.

In our reckless acts, time seems to slow to a crawl. Oh, they still ultimately rush past you like bullets, but in the moment your experience of them is strangely dilated, so a single second is experienced in slow motion. After I jumped, I sailed through the air for what felt like an eternity. The bottom of the robe swept upward so that I was like some flying version of Marilyn Monroe and my balls were revealed to the world. In that crisp night, my balls glinted in the perfect light of a full moon and there was some mystical conjunction or glimmer of divinity. Or maybe it was the most perfect movie poster... which I guess would have some sort of an X-rating.

But that moment was an apex, just the high point in a journey that descended rapidly. Frantically I grabbed at the hem of the robe, trying to desperately cover my family jewels as the bushes surged towards me. I hoped against all realism that I'd simply strike the bushes and bounce off, slightly scraped and unharmed. I closed my eyes and hoped.

I believe it was Nietzsche that said that "Hope in reality is the worst of all evils because it prolongs the torments of man." All I know is that hope did not prevent the torment of my balls.

I remember striking the tops of the bushes, their claws grasping up at me like the ravenous dead. That alone hurt. But a moment later, the force of my descent and my own weight had weakened the branches enough that they broke and I fell down *into* a bush. Where before I had brushed up against the ends of the top branches, weaker and brittle, now my poor nethers scraped across strong inner branches, thick and nearly unbreakable.

For just a moment after the fall, I sat in the bush, the shock of it overriding anything else, the bizarreness of the predicament telegraphed across my mind. But such anesthesia lasted just a moment. Then I screamed. I screamed loud and with all my being. My scream was that of a man who had not only felt excruciating pain, but had suffered such torment at the core of his being, in the one part where his hopes, his love, and his consciousness rested. My balls. Like the cutting of Sampson's hair, this attack on my most treasured region was a darker attack on my soul than any mere attempt on my life would create. I admit that after I screamed, I wept for a few moments.

I knew I had to get out of that bush, but I knew further friction would add more pain. So with gentle movements and a wincing expression, I lifted my posterior from the hellish claws of the bush and pushed myself forward. I gingerly pushed myself over the lip of the unbroken branches and fell forward onto the grass, free of that torturous bush.

I lay face down gasping for breath. When my wits returned to me, I turned over and assessed the damage.

Scratches covered my legs and crotch. I looked as if I were a man who attempted love making with a dryad to discover that her feminine nature only went so far. My balls were scratched, yes, but thankfully not bloody. My thighs were the worst case: they each had long scratches that even now dripped blood. I pulled a few large splinters of wood out of them with a hiss..

As I stood up, I realized that while my legs were shaky and the scratches stung, I had not broken any bones. I looked back up at the roof to see the distance I had jumped, but my blood ran cold. On the roof staring down at me was Sally.

She had a look of hate and frenzy, but her eyes were half lidded as if in the throes of some strange pleasure. She still held the knife and had not bothered to dress, so she stood naked on the roof in the moonlight, looking like some vicious Bacchae.

We stared at each other. Unless she went back into the house or made the jump into the bushes herself, she had no way of reaching me. She knew that I had escaped and was not pleased. I knew I had triumphed in my escape, though I had paid for it in desperate pain.

It was I who broke our stare. I turned and ran, not wanting to risk her ire or to dare her to take the plunge into the bushes to chase me. In a hobbling run, I charged off into the night, leaving her staring after me, armed and naked in the wind and moonlight.

* * *

An hour later I arrived back at Sally's house in a police squad car.

After my jump I had limped to a busy nearby road. While none of the helpful motorists seemed willing to stop and pick up a scratched and limping man in a too small frilly pink bathrobe, they were more than willing to dial 911. For the cops, a naked man in a pink bathrobe was just par for the course.

Back at the police station, I had a great deal of explaining to do. The idea that I was an adjunct professor or a male underwear model seemed unlikely to them. The idea that I could be both seemed an impossibility which made me look even credible. I was left alone in the interrogation room a few times where I looked at the scratches on my legs. When they applied disinfectants from the first aid kit, I had nearly howled in pain. Now they only throbbed in a dull pain. I wondered how long the scratches would keep me from photo shoots.

Ultimately, they found they didn't have a good reason to hold me. They had nothing to charge me with; there was no alcohol in my system, and despite the robe being too small, it did actually cover my junk as long as there was not a strong breeze blowing. My case was probably helped by the fact that I did sort of look like the picture on the website for my lecture, though I was clearly far more disheveled now.

From that point, they were obligated to look into my claims of attempted murder. They assumed it was more likely a domestic disturbance rather than murder in the face of all my protests. But if it got me a ride and police escort back to my pants, I was not going to complain. I received a pair of police-issue sweat pants to wear and the assurance that they would never want that pair back.

I was very adverse to walking up to the door of Sally's house, but the officer told me under no terms was I allowed to stay in the squad car, even if I had pants now. I wondered if he thought I was going to teabag the seats. I just didn't want to get stabbed.

It took a few knocks on the door and the loud statement that they were police before Sally finally opened it, looking sheepish and not at all insane. She had dressed in simple pajamas and didn't look at all like she had been banging a professor nor like she had followed him out on the roof to stab him just an hour ago.

Though she might have been able to lie about all of it, she didn't. I think she was shocked to have the police at her door, or maybe she had come down off her insanity. Or maybe she just feared that they'd get a warrant and discover more than she wanted. She didn't disavow all knowledge of me and admitted that I had been there. However, she was shocked at any claims of an attack, doing her best acting job. Since they couldn't prove I had been attacked and I had no wounds other than those inflicted by the bushes, the attempted murder angle was dropped and any pretense of her being a suspect disappeared. The officer who was allowed inside found my clothes and my wallet, so I finally received respect first for not being a liar and second for actually being a university professor. I tried to show them some of my wallet photos of my best underwear shoots, but they were uninterested.

Another squad car was called to take me back to the university. The first officer stayed at Sally's to take a statement from her. I hope his balls are okay.

With a sigh, I sunk back into the cushions of the second squad car's backseat. I carried my folded jeans and underwear with my left arm; nobody wanted to give me any leeway to be naked again, even if it was just to change out of the police sweat pants. My shirt tugged uncomfortably on me, as I had put that on in a hurry, so I kept fidgeting in my seat.

The officer in this squad car kept staring at me in the rear view as we drove towards the university. I was hoping she wasn't going to pull a knife on me too, but she finally spoke.

"So I hear that you're an underwear model."

I smiled. Things were getting back to normal. I knew where this was going.

"Yes, that's right," I said.

"I've always wondered about the men in those magazines," she said. "You always hear about female underwear models, but not the men." She paused, catching herself. "I'm sorry, you've had a rough night. Do you mind the questions?"

"Not at all," I said. "I'm always willing to answer the questions of a fan."

In the rear view, I saw her smile. "Oh really? I've always really wondered, but all those male models... I guess what I'm asking..." She paused. "Do you have to manscape your balls?"

Dane Monday Saves Christmas (With Help)

Author's Note

The events of this story occur after the second Nowak Brothers novel, *Jabberwock Jack,* and the second Dane Monday novel, *Burning Monday.* This story spoils neither, nor is any knowledge of previous novels really needed. Also, the time frame which this story occurs wouldn't actually be December, but like all good Holiday Specials, the opportunity for a cheap Christmas cash-in warps all space and time to do its bidding. Happy Holidays!

1

"So I'm not sure if I buy this whole Santa Claus thing," said Dane Monday, investigator of weird occurrences, thwarter of villains, and mediocre poker player. He threw down his cards. "Fold."

"What's there to 'buy'?" said Jaya, technophile, robotic expert, and car mechanic. Her cards were fanned out in her hands in front of her and her feet up on the table. She was smoking a cigar.

"Don't get me wrong, you know I'm a big fan of Christmas. But I've always wondered about Santa. Y'know, the whole Saint Nick living at the North Pole and delivering all his toys through magical means once a year," said Dane. "What if it's not magic or the supernatural? What if he's just some guy using Avalon Brass inventions?"

"It's possible," said Jaya. "But why discount magic? What would be so strange about the existence of a mythic figure that supposedly uses magic to do good things for the world? You deal with works of magic and fantastic things all the time. You see the 'impossible' on a daily basis."

"Yeah," said Wong. "I'm a fox." Wong was a Chinese fox spirit who masqueraded as a human.

"And even if you want to say it's all Brass, who cares?" said Jaya. "Why would that change things?"

Alastair coughed from Jaya's cigar smoke, which always seemed to waft straight toward him. An old school occultist, he was dressed down from his usual impeccable attire. He was not wearing his usual blazer, but he still had a crisp white shirt and red-and-green striped tie for the holiday. His sleeves were rolled up to his arm garters. "And the figure of Saint Nicholas has existed for centuries. A single individual would likely have died from old age if nothing occult was involved." He pause and looked at his cards. "I call."

"What if it's a succession of people?" said Dane. "Some hereditary title and set of gear passed on through the years."

"A long line of Santa Clauses back to medieval times?" said Jaya. "I guess it could be plausible, but Avalon Brass wasn't found back then. And not in Europe."

"It could have and we don't know it," said Dane. "Linda, what do you think?"

Linda, a university history professor, did not hear Dane, as she was in the kitchen, which currently was a warzone. Since she did not play poker but had arrived for the Christmas Eve celebration, she had been baking cookies for everyone in the small apartment kitchen. But this was Wong's home and his wife, Meilin, also a fox spirit, was not taking kindly to the interloper in her kitchen. They were currently arguing.

Instead, Dane was answered by Abby. An aspiring journalist and Dane's latest sidekick, she was sitting at the small bar near the kitchen. Next to her was a small folding table where Dane had placed the numerous Christmas hams he had arranged to have delivered for everyone. Nobody was excited about their gift hams, but Dane was very excited to give them as it was his traditional holiday gift, so they did not say anything. They'd all take them home, put them in their refrigerators, pick at them for a week, then throw them out. Just like every year.

"I think she's maybe a little busy," said Abby. Since she also did not play poker but was not attempting to bake, Abby had nothing to do but sit around and drink while she enjoyed everyone's company. This meant she had drank a little more than everyone else. She was only drinking eggnog spiked with brandy, but she had so much that she was already somewhat red faced and clumsy.

"Husband, would you get this crazy white woman out of my kitchen?" shouted Meilin in exasperation.

"I'm just trying to bake!" said Linda in exasperation, oven mitts on her hands, her fifth batch of cookies on a tray in her arms, and white flour on her nose. She wore a far-too festive holiday sweater, an endless amount of green, red, and white Americana.

"Husband, do something!" said Meilin.

"Dane," said Wong, turning from his cards, "please tell Honorable Wife that I am in the middle of a game, trying to win moneys for our family."

Dane didn't say anything but turned to Meilin with a *what-can-I-do* gesture that was half shrug and half supplication. Meilin asking Wong to do things during the regular poker games was a time-worn fight between the two of them.

"Dane," counted Meilin, "please tell Honorable Husband that if this white woman does not get out of my kitchen, I will break my centuries-old vow against killing." No one mentioned how recent events may have called that vow into question.

"I'm just trying to bake for everyone," said Linda, her voice weak and sad. It was more than just being unappreciated. She didn't want to get killed by an angry fox spirit either. She just wanted to bake cookies for everyone.

Wong sighed and put down his cards. "I guess I'll have to fold."

"We can wait if you want," said Jaya, blowing a smoke ring. "That way we can get your money fairly."

CTHULHU, PRIVATE INVESTIGATOR & OTHER STORIES   171

"I would find that acceptable - ow!" said Alastair, reaching down to rub his ankle.

"Meilin, the kids are awake and got out of their room again!" said Wong, looking under the table. Then he carefully got up and bent under the table. His children, Yuju and Lili, were so young that they did not know how to shift their shape. So instead of appearing as human children, they were two red fox cubs with white stripes. In addition to getting in all sorts of trouble, they liked biting people's ankles under the table. For some reason they particularly liked biting Alastair's legs.

Meilin quickly left the kitchen and crouched by the poker table. "I have Lili!" she said, scooping a small fox up in her arms.

"I've got Yuju!" said Wong, stroking the small fox's chin. "Who's a mischievous little monster? Is it you? Is it you?"

"I kind of feel like you'd be that sort of parent," said Jaya to Dane.

"If I had monster babies?" said Dane.

"They're not monsters," said Meilin.

"No, I think he's correct," said Wong, receiving a dirty look from his wife. He smiled.

"No, I mean -" started Jaya, but she didn't get to finish. Suddenly the unused cards on the table jumped into the air. They swirled together in a momentary dust devil. They all saw this and stared in shock. But Dane saw more. In the middle of that swirl of cards he saw a sight that was strange but appropriate for the day - Santa Claus.

Then the cards fell to the table as quickly as they arose, the strange phenomenon and Dane's vision gone.

"Okay, what was that?" said Jaya.

"A localized psychokinetic event," said Alastair. He clutched at a necklace under his shirt. "It's not demonic or angelic. I would know."

"My kids haven't learned that trick yet," said Wong defensively.

"It's a case, isn't it, Dane?" said Abby, her voice a little slurred.

Dane nodded. "Yeah, I saw something in all that. A vision. Something I need to go take care of."

"But it's Christmas Eve!" said Jaya. "Don't you get a night off? It's midnight already."

"Evil doesn't take a night off, so neither should I," said Dane.

Nobody said anything for a moment. Then they started laughing.

"I can't believe you said that with a straight face," said Jaya, wiping tears.

"Seriously, what movies have you been watching?" said Wong.

"Okay, the point is, if I'm getting a message, I still need to go," said Dane finishing his mug and then standing up. "I've also had like five cups of coffee, so I'm good for the night. Abby, you coming with?"

"I've had a little too much to drink, I think," said Abby, lifting her mug to see it was empty again. "I also told Will I'd stay put until he picked me up. Which seems like a good idea right now."

"Your government agent boyfriend is coming *here*?" said Jaya. She looked over to Dane, who was a person of interest in various arsons around town, then at the two human-looking but non-human fox spirits, and finally at Alastair, who was known for some under the table dealings for occult objects. She did not even mention her own technically illegal salvaging runs to the Husks and elsewhere. She guessed only Linda wouldn't be a person of interest for the government agent.

"Oh, no, I'm going to meet him around the block," said Abby. "He'll call when he's here."

"Ask him if he got his ham," said Dane.

Abby rolled her eyes and then watched Dane get his coat on over his Christmas sweater. "Be careful, they're saying it could get as bad as a blizzard out there."

"Evil doesn't take a night -" began Dane again.

"Just go," said Jaya.

2

Not far away across New Avalon, the mood wasn't as nearly as warm and festive. The Christmas spirit was lacking in at least one individual.

"So that's why I think Christmas isn't worthwhile," said Szandor Nowak, unlicensed monster hunter and lifetime curmudgeon, age twenty-one.

"Come off it, brother," said Mikkel Nowak, unlicensed monster hunter and his brother's keeper, age twenty-three. "This is not the time of year to be cynical. You're being a Scrooge."

"I'm just saying that Christmas seems like a rich person holiday," said Szandor, a glass that was now empty of whiskey in his hand. "A consumer holiday. It's about buying stuff for your families, buying tons of food, and purchasing terrible Christmas decorations. If you don't buy, you are left out."

"The commercialization of Christmas is a relatively new thing, historically speaking," said Carly, Mikkel's girlfriend. She spent more time here at Mikkel's apartment than at her own, so the fact that she was spending Christmas with the Nowak brothers wasn't surprising. Especially since she wasn't always fond of her own family.

"See?" said Mikkel. "It wasn't always like this. Maybe things got out of hand, but it's still a time for family and friends. Loved ones. Goodwill toward men. That kind of stuff."

"I don't have a lot of goodwill to give," said Szandor. "This wasn't my year." It had been a rough year for him. He was still dealing with the lingering emotions that come from nearly dying from a traumatic fight that had put him in a coma. The fact that he was getting abusive calls from collections agencies about his hospital bills added insult to injury.

"I get that, brother, but the important thing is we're both alive. We have each other, and that's how Mom would have wanted it. You know how important Christmas was to her," said Mikkel.

Szandor nodded faintly. Their mother had always done the best to make their Christmas as good as she could, but money was often tight. Their holidays were nothing like the ones Szandor saw on television, with their impressive decorations, the family sprawled out in front of the fire and the tree, a huge roasted goose or turkey with enough for unexpected guests, and everyone getting their Christmas wish. Szandor could count on one hand the times he had ever gotten the present he wanted. He understood why that was back then and he understood even more why now as an adult, but sometimes the old hurts are unreasonable. He still carried a strong feeling of disappointment for the whole holiday.

He looked over to his brother and Carly who were laying on the couch, her head resting on Mikkel's chest as they watched The Christmas Story on the television. Szandor was a little envious. He had been moving from one odd job to another, perpetually single, and had almost been killed by a gigantic serpent. Not a good year. Mikkel, however, had been reunited with his probable one true love. That seemed like a much better year. Okay, Szandor admitted, so maybe his brother also saved Szandor's life. Szandor still felt like he always got the short end of the stick. Things never went his way.

The bad feelings crawling up in him, he suddenly felt like he didn't want to be here with the loving couple. He wanted to be elsewhere, somewhere he could breathe. He also didn't want to spoil their holiday. If he was going to be a jerk to someone, as typically happened when he started feeling bad, better that be someone other than his brother.

"I'm gonna get going," said Szandor, rising from the armchair. Most of the whiskey had worn off and he felt something resembling sober.

Mikkel shook his head in disappointment. "You're welcome to stay, the snow might get bad on your way home."

Szandor shook his head in disagreement. "No, I'm fine. The snow is fine. I think I just want to be alone."

Mikkel opened his mouth to say something about being alone on Christmas, but then he looked to Carly and back to his brother. He got it. Even with his only family, Szandor must have been feeling a little bit like a third wheel.

"You're coming over tomorrow, right?" said Mikkel. "Can you drop by the store and get a can of cranberries for the sauce? We forgot to get that at the store."

"I don't know if I'm coming over," said Szandor.

"Oh, come on, we'll have food. Lem will be over after he finishes at his aunt's. You can bring Dickie. We'll have alcohol and drink until we're stupid."

"Dickie's out of town for the holiday," said Szandor.

"Well, still come over," said Mikkel. "Carly's sister is invited, so she might come. She's cute."

"Eh," said Carly with a lazy shrug. "If you like that sort of thing."

"You're not really selling it, brother," said Szandor.

"Brother," said Mikkel very seriously. "I would really like it if you came over and spent Christmas with me. And all of us. It would mean a lot to me for you to be there."

Szandor sighed. "I just don't think it's a good thing."

"Spending time with family is always a good thing," said Mikkel.

"Maybe I'm sick of family," said Szandor angrily.

"Maybe you *do* need to spend some time alone tonight," said Mikkel in a too hasty retort.

"Are you kicking me out now?" said Szandor.

"What the hell, guys?" said Carly.

Mikkel sighed and shook his head slowly. "I'm sorry. Look, brother, do what you need to tonight. Maybe you'll be less of a jerk tomorrow."

Szandor did not answer, he just shook his head and left, his heart still full of anger.

3

When Szandor hit the street, it was snowing. Not a blizzard or at least not one yet, but enough snow that the streets were thinning of people. Of course, it was late at night on Christmas Eve - most people were home with their families. Those that weren't were closing out the night at their favorite bar, so they still had a few hours to go before stumbling out onto the street.

Szandor wasn't dressed for the snow. He wore his jacket, but he didn't have a hat nor gloves. Admittedly the jacket was not meant for very cold weather either. He pulled the sleeves of the jacket down and wrapped his hands around them, holding them in place. He realized that he had a bad habit of leaving places too quickly while ill prepared for the weather outside.

Mikkel lived in Chinatown, so as Szandor walked toward home, he was seeing the odd mix of Chinese advertisement and Christmas decorations. Sometimes he saw both, like when he saw a neon green Christmas tree covered with orange neon Chinese characters. Much of Chinatown had been rebuilt since recent fires, so there was a mix between new construction, old buildings, and just a few places that still showed fire damage. As he walked on, Szandor saw a familiar sight during the holidays: a volunteer Santa collecting donations for charity.

The man was dressed in a cheap red Santa suit, the white trim missing in places. His beard was poorly made, looking to be made up of cotton balls. He was standing in front of a big cauldron where people could toss in donations. He didn't have a sign saying the Salvation Army or any other charity; there was nothing to identify who he worked for. On the ground next to the cauldron was a red sack typical of Santa. His arm swung a bell rhythmically, up and down, up and down, never failing in the exact repetition. His voice also had a very specific rhythm to it, always saying, "Ho ho ho!" at just the right pitch and interval.

Szandor had to walk past the charity Santa, but he did so with a distaste that rose from his current anger and longstanding disappointment with the holiday.

"Ho ho ho!"

"Not interested," said Szandor.

Then as he was just past the Santa: "Ho ho ho!"

"I said I'm not interested!"

Then when he had finally walked away: "Ho ho ho!"

Szandor whipped around. The Santa was looking right at him, but he couldn't discern any real emotion in the Santa's face, probably because of the fake beard. Szandor considered going off on the Santa, letting out some of that pent-up frustration. But he thought better of it, realizing that even he didn't want to be the guy who got into a fight with a charity Santa on Christmas Eve. He'd never live that down even if the police didn't show up.

Instead he turned back around and decided to mind his own business. He ignored the additional "Ho ho ho!" behind him, though he really wanted to go back and punch the annoying Santa in his stupid face. Instead, he kept his self control and kept on walking.

He was so concentrated on keeping his temper and not turning around to attack the Santa that he was caught completely unaware when someone grabbed him and pulled him into an alley. As he was pushed against the wall, he decided now he could finally let loose. He raised his fists, then frowned. He recognized his attacker.

"It's you!" said Szandor in confusion.

"Shhh," said the other man, peering toward the alley entrance.

"You're that Day of the Week guy, uh, Dave Tuesday!" said Szandor. He relaxed, as he had met this man before. He was weird, but at least Szandor knew he could easily take him in a fight.

"That's *Dane Monday*," said Dane. "But yes, it's me! I didn't know you would be here! Did you get a good look at that Santa? Did he attack you?"

"The charity Santa?" said Szandor. "No. He's just a volunteer charity worker. He doesn't attack people. He could be drunk, I guess, but otherwise they're not violent. It was more a concern of whether I was going to attack him."

"Oh, so you know already!" said Dane with relief.

"Know what?"

"That he's not Santa!" said Dane.

"Uh, yeah, I know he's not the real Santa Claus," said Szandor. "I know there's no real Santa Claus..."

"Well, maybe there is," said Dane, thinking back to the conversation earlier in the night, "but that's not important right now! I'm saying he's not a real... what was it you said? He's not a charity Santa!"

Szandor stepped toward the alley entrance and carefully looked toward the Santa. The charity worker was still standing in the same spot, endlessly ringing the bell and repeating, "Ho ho ho!" even though there was no one near him. Szandor admitted that was sort of weird. "So what are you thinking," said Szandor. "Mugger? Gangster? I think I could be down with hitting a mugger in the face on Christmas Eve. That might even make my holiday."

"That Santa is no mugger," said Dane with surprising gravity.

"Then what?" said Szandor in exasperation. "Do I have to guess what he is?"

"He's a robot!" said Dane.

Szandor stared at Dane in disbelief for a moment. "I think I liked it better when I was guessing."

"He is! Look at the very exact and perfect repetition of his ringing! Like clockwork! And listen to his voice! The same audio each time!"

"That dude could just be really into being exact," said Szandor. "Like some obsessive compulsive thing. Or he's... I don't know, some mental illness. That doesn't make him a robot. That's actually kind of insulting to him."

"Those are just the more obvious signs," said Dane. "Under that cheap suit and beard, he's just a mechanical automaton. I'm sure of it."

"Look, I know you got your own thing going on and stuff, and that's cool," said Szandor, "but I just really don't see the robot thing."

"I'll just say that I have experience with this. Tell you what, if I can reveal that it is a robot, can you take it down? I know you can handle yourself in aggressive situations. I normally am not big on violence, but since it's just a robot..."

"Whoa, we're going straight to robot killing?" said Szandor. "That's an abrupt change. And I'm not really equipped for fighting, I just came from my brother's apartment..."

"Oh, so you're not armed," said Dane disappointedly. "I guess I might have something in my bag..."

"Oh, I'm armed alright," said Szandor. He had a lead pipe down the back of his jacket in a makeshift sheath stitched into the lining. It was a shorter and thinner lead pipe, but it was far more damaging than his fists. "Too many damn monsters in this town. And *maybe* I'm worried I've pissed off the wrong people."

"I know the feeling!" said Dane, but Szandor guessed their experiences were far different.

"But I'm not carrying anything big or very lethal," said Szandor. "I mean, robots are steel and sturdy, right?"

"You'd be surprised how prone to injury the average robot is! They're rarely built for endurance! You'll do fine!" said Dane, patting Szandor on the back. "Right, so when you see it's a robot, come out swinging... or hitting.. or whatever's appropriate!"

Dane then launched himself out of the alley toward the robot before Szandor had a chance to say anything. *It's a really vague plan,* thought Szandor, *but I guess I've worked with worse.* He pulled the lead pipe out and crouched at the alley entrance.

Walking quickly toward the Santa, Dane had the luck of coming at him from the side. The Santa was still endlessly ringing his bell and chanting "Ho ho ho!" but there was no one near him, so he stared out into the emptiness of the street, almost looking sad and depressed. But Dane knew better.

The Santa began to turn as Dane trotted toward him. Brushing by him, Dane yanked at the beard and hat, pulling them off as he ran a few paces away from the red-clad form. The removal of these items revealed a smooth head and a blank face. The Santa had a blank metal head not unlike a department store mannequin. Someone had given it real-looking eyes and painted the top of its face flesh colored, but had been lazy and did not paint the top of its head once hidden by the hat nor the mouth section hidden by the beard.

"Look, it's a robot! Clearly a robot!" shouted Dane as he stood away from it, still holding the fake beard and hat.

The robot not-Santa turned to look at Dane. Something clicked behind its eyes, those pupils now looking very inhuman.

"DANE MONDAY IDENTIFIED," said the robot.

"Oh, do we... uh, know each other?" said Dane.

The robot raised both its arms. This meant that one arm looked threatening while the other was simply ringing the bell at a higher height.

Then there was the sound of footsteps running across pavement in the night, the sound becoming louder. The robot paused for a second and looked as if it was going to turn. Then there was a loud clang as Szandor's pipe struck its head. The metal robot head went flying, finally coming down loudly somewhere across the street. At the robot Santa's neck were a collection of sparking wires. The bell stopped ringing.

"Did I kill it? Is it dead?" shouted Szandor, hopped up on adrenaline. "Do I need to hit it again?"

Dane squinted his eyes at the body of the robot. Aside from the sparking wires, there was no activity. The arms were frozen in a raised position. Without the head, Dane had no way of knowing if it was shouting death threats at him. He slowly stepped closer, ready to jump if it made any movement. Finally he reached out with his hand and pushed. The robot body fell to the ground with a noise muffled by the felt of the cheap Santa suit.

"Yeah, we're safe," said Dane, bending down to examine the robot.

"I didn't mean to behead it," said Szandor, still hyped on adrenaline and looking down at his lead pipe. "I thought maybe I'd just dent the head or bash in its skull... robot skull, I guess. But man, did you see how much air time I got on that head?"

Dane nodded absentmindedly as he unbuckled the robot's suit and opened up the access panel. "So what do we have in here? Motor systems, processor. No notable armaments. This all looks very familiar but it's still not my area of expertise. I could call Jaya, but it's Christmas Eve, she needs a night off. Maybe if I could... hmmm..."

"Did you need me to actually answer any of that mumbling?" said Szandor. He was looking in the charity cauldron. He found it surprisingly devoid of money other than a few coins. He found that the red Santa sack contained a few wrapped presents. There were no recipients written on the tags. "Looks like Christmas came early for me!" said Szandor with a smile as he started tearing the wrapping of one.

Dane rubbed his chin. "Robot Santa, just what were you for? What was the plan? I don't think the charities simply decided to automate the donation process for the holiday. What were you supposed to do?"

"Blow stuff up," said Szandor.

"What?" said Dane, looking up from the robot.

Szandor was holding a half ripped present, revealing a strange device. It had buttons and wires, but also a display where it could show a digital time. There were different colored wires, including the dreaded red wire. "I'm not tech geek like you, but I'm pretty sure I know an explosive device when I see one. There are half a dozen other presents in here. I'm pretty sure Robot Santa was going to blow stuff up. A lot of stuff."

"But why?" said Dane. "There's nothing around here!"

"My brother lives around here, there's not nothing around here."

"A good friend of mine lives around here too," said Dane. "I meant there are no worthwhile targets for a..."

"Robot Santa?" suggested Szandor.

"I was thinking Mad Bomber," said Dane. "Someone was controlling the robot. But why?"

"What if it's not the only robot?" said Szandor. "This time of year, charity Santas are on every damn street corner. A few more robot ones and nobody would notice... well, except the real charity Santas, and they might be too nice to complain about losing territory."

"Street corners all over the city..." said Dane, realization dawning on him. "It's a massive attack on Christmas Eve while everyone is enjoying the holiday! Someone's trying to destroy the city!"

"Really?" said Szandor. "People try to do that?"

"They have in my experience," said Dane.

"But this wouldn't destroy the city," said Szandor. "Bombs might hurt some people and collapse a few buildings, but most of the city would survive. You'd need so many of these Santas that they'd be pretty obvious. We'd notice an excess of charity Santas."

"It's worse than I thought!" said Dane. "They're trying to hurt Christmas!"

"That's worse than the city being destroyed?" said Szandor, but he felt like Dane wasn't seriously listening to him.

"Explosions all over the city, chaos for the holidays! Someone wants to attack the spirit of Christmas itself!"

"I... guess? Are we really doing this?" said Szandor.

"We have to find them and stop them!" said Dane. "Are you with me, Szandor?"

"Sure...? I guess I don't have anything else going on tonight."

"Then we need to find the villain's lair and stop them!" said Dane. Then he looked down into the guts of the Santa Robot. He pulled out one piece of machinery. "This is the transponder! It's what sends and receives the signal from its home base. We can use this to find its headquarters!"

"Does it have a map or GPS we can use?" said Szandor, looking at the device in Dane's hands. It looked like someone's wifi router with some of the wires torn out.

"No, but I have a signal tracker I can connect to it which will lead us back to its source!" said Dane, rifling around in his bag.

"And you just happen to be carrying a signal tracker with you?" said Szandor.

"Yes! Why, don't you carry stuff like that?" said Dane, trying to figure out which wire to connect to the transponder, finally deciding to connect all the wires and hope for the best.

"I feel like I'm in some outlandish dream," said Szandor.

"Yes, an outlandish dream where we save Christmas!" said Dane.

"I may strangle you by the end of the night," said Szandor.

"It looks like the signal is coming from someplace up in Asher!" said Dane. He picked up the sack full of bombs. "Let's get a cab!"

"We're taking bombs with us? Why are we taking bombs with us?"

"So no one else can use them of course!" said Dane.

"I don't trust you with bombs," said Szandor, grabbing the sack from Dane and throwing it over his shoulder. "I don't think we should be carrying explosive devices, but if one of us is carrying them, I think it should be me. I might be reckless, but I think you're crazy."

"Ah, a common opinion," said Dane.

4

The cab let them off in Asher at some time after two in the morning. It had taken longer than usual, the cab moving slowly through the snow covered streets. During this time the cab driver explained his own Hindu beliefs under the waxing holiday of another religious system, something Dane listened to with interest and Szandor ignored. The driver didn't question the giant sack of presents and Szandor made damn sure he didn't suspect there was actually a large amount of bombs riding around in his cab. Szandor also hoped there wasn't a remote activation for the bombs, or else all three of them and the cab would be vaporized.

Dane paused to pay the cab driver, so Szandor was the first to step out of cab, lugging the sack full of bombs. Dane found Szandor staring up at the building, a confused look on his face.

"Are you sure this is the place?" said Szandor.

Dane pulled out his signal tracker. He punched a button, heard a strange electronic sound, nodded, then put it away. "Yup, this is the place!"

"It's a cat food warehouse," said Szandor.

A giant neon sign over the building said *Meow Brand Cat Food* in dull red letters. White flashing letters lit up the brand slogan *nom Nom NOM!* periodically. Other than the sign, it looked like a quiet building, marred by the years, graffiti on some of the walls. However, there were trucks at the loading docks and it looked like some of the docks were open, a strange sight for late at night on Christmas Eve. They did not see any workers, however.

"Yes, warehouses are a popular haunt for villains!" said Dane. "Usually more for mad scientists and master criminals, but the odd demon or diabolist will use an old warehouse too! Though I guess it's a popular lair type in general - kind of the all purpose default. But if we're here, then odds are it's a mad scientist or master criminal! I guess either of them could have a grudge against Christmas! We'll find out soon!"

"I can't tell which bothers me more, that everything with you has some strong internal logic, like it's all a well constructed game - like, 'of course mad scientists are popular renters of warehouses'," said Szandor, "or the fact that you are like totally getting off on all this. The next time someone accuses me of having a danger fetish, I'm going to give them your number and tell them to hang out with you for a while before judging me."

"I think you've just lost your zest for life," said Dane. "You have your own dangerous situations. You can either enter them in fear or you enter them in wonder. But either way, we both know we're going to be involved, right?"

Szandor scowled, but there was some sense to what he said. "So how are we going to be involved in this one?"

Dane pointed to one of the open loading docks, the entrance unguarded. "I find that when I see an open door, I use it."

"And into certain doom we go," said Szandor. He threw the sack of bomb-presents over his other shoulder and pulled out his lead pipe.

Dane climbed up onto the loading dock, looking into the building. Though there was no snow inside the warehouse, it was no warmer than the outside. Dane wondered how any of the late night workers or henchmen of the mystery mad scientist or master criminal would be comfortable. Then he realized that wasn't a concern.

"Robots!" said Szandor. Dane immediately clapped his hand over Szandor's mouth and pulled the younger man to the side behind some crates. A pair of robots stomped past them, heading to the loading dock. They grabbed a crate and walked it back into the warehouse.

The two heroes looked over the crates at the rest of the warehouse. From here they could see the whole setup. Robots walked to and fro, performing various tasks, usually lifting and moving, but a few were interfacing with consoles. None were dressed to look like Santa Claus. While a few had green elf hats over their siren-like heads, they were generally unadorned. Their gray metal forms only had a single designation: R-39.

In the center of the warehouse was the main staging area. One half of it was devoted to a large red sleigh. It was much like the traditional Santa's sleigh, but modified with technology and violent intent. There were exhausts and engines that were more similar to hover jets or rockets, as well as a swivel gun turret on the back. Missiles were attached to its underside. The reindeer in front of it were clearly mechanical, showing off their own jet engines. The robots were loading a large bag of gifts into the sleigh.

The other half of the warehouse's staging area was a gigantic bank of monitors and consoles. As Dane and Szandor watched, they saw maps of the city showing about two dozen locations. Dane guessed these were the other Robot Santas. This was clearly where they were controlled from. And in front of the consoles was a high backed chair - Dane was unsurprised, villains always loved high backed chairs. When the chair spun around so that the villain could survey the work on the sleigh, Dane knew him in an instant. He was wearing a heavy Santa suit without the hat or fake white beard, but Dane still knew that dark beard and stern expression.

"Professor Honnenheim," said Dane icily.

"Professor?" said Szandor. "You know this guy from college?"

Dane shook his head. "We have tangled before. He wants to take over the city. He's attempted it a few times but failed. Don't you remember the North Egan destruction? He's partly responsible."

"That was him?" said Szandor in sudden anger. "Alright, this guy is going down!" Szandor began standing up, his grip tight on the lead pipe.

Dane grabbed Szandor. "Hold on, there are R-39s everywhere! We need a plan! Or some semblance of one!"

"I've got a sack full of bombs," suggested Szandor.

"That's good, that will help," said Dane, rubbing his chin. "But how to stop him without the robots destroying us?"

"Get real lucky?" said Szandor.

"Wait, I've got it," said Dane. "How much do you trust me?"

5

Professor Honnenheim watched the displays. His Robot Santas were all in place. The sleigh was nearly loaded. Soon he would be able to start his assault. He knew it would go down in history as the Avalon Christmas Assault or the New Avalon Holiday Tragedy. It wouldn't get him any farther on his plan to take over the city, but it would put a big dent in this infernal holiday. *Goodwill toward men indeed*, he scoffed.

Suddenly all the screens popped up with the same message. It was echoed by the voices of the R-39 units all around him. "DANE MONDAY IDENTIFIED."

Honnenheim swung around in his chair to see the familiar form of Dane Monday in front of him - smug face, satchel, and today wearing an ugly Christmas Sweater under his coat. Dane stood only a few paces from the chair, the robots knowing Dane was a special case and waiting for Honnenheim's orders to fire. Dane held in his hands one of the Christmas present bombs.

"I expected I should have to deal with you," said Honnenheim tiredly. "When I received an identification signal from the Chinatown Santa right before it went offline, I knew you were catching on. I had hoped to take off before you arrived, but I see that luck has failed me. You always show up."

"Like a bad penny!" said Dane cheerfully.

"I suppose the bomb is so I do not have my R-39s kill you immediately?" said Honnenheim.

"Yes, I figured I'd want some insurance in case you didn't feel like monologuing."

"You do realize that all the bombs are remotely activated, right? From this very console, in fact," said the Professor, waving at his setup.

"You're welcome to try setting it off right now," said Dane, "though at this proximity I think we're both going to have a terrible Christmas. But I'll let you in on a secret: you can't set off or shut down this bomb. I changed the frequency before revealing myself. We've done this dance before, we both know how each other thinks." Truthfully, Dane hadn't had the time or tools to change the frequency. He had only jammed a screwdriver into the bomb and twisted it around, hoping that would deactivate it. Under no circumstances would he actually want it to explode in his hands.

"You have no idea how much the dance is beginning to bore me," said Honnenheim.

"Really? You're usually so excited for all this! Has the Holiday gotten you down? Where's your Christmas spirit?"

"Christmas is a holiday for fools," said Honnenheim. "So are Chanukah and Solstice gatherings! All the winter holidays are foolish traditions!"

"What about Kwanza?"

"Everyone thinks they are safe on Christmas," said Honnenheim. "They act like the world will just stop so they can take off a day to be with their families. They think goodwill and cheer will change everything when it won't change anything. Not this year. Avalon will know true terror. A burning terror." Honnenheim lapsed into a sullen look.

"Isn't this the part where you laugh maniacally?" said Dane.

"I am in no mood for mirth," said Honnenheim.

"Wow, worse than I thought," said Dane. "I'd say we need to teach you the true meaning of Christmas, but I don't think there's enough Charlie Brown television specials for that."

"Your playfulness is particularly unappreciated today, Monday."

"PREPARATIONS COMPLETE," said a robot.

Honnenheim nodded and swiveled around to the consoles. He looked up at one then pressed a few buttons. A section of the ceiling opened up loudly, snow coming through the gap. The noise of a scuffle from the other side of the warehouse was lost in that sound. Then he pressed another set of buttons and turned back around. "Your bomb is now deactivated. I am disappointed at the bluff, Monday. Did you think I couldn't see the signal on my displays? I would be able to see that the frequency was changed and the bomb missing."

"Oh, you know, sometimes time is short," said Dane. "You have to improvise."

"Indeed," said Honnenheim. "Robots, kill him."

"Wait!" said Dane, putting out his hand in front of him.

"Oh, what pathetic Monday plot is it now?" said Honnenheim.

"I brought help. You're in danger. Kill me and you'll suffer their wrath."

Honnenheim sat back in his chair with an annoyed sigh. "Who is it? The red haired girl? That traitor Jaya? I appreciate that you see worth in them, but neither is particularly dangerous. The girl is harmless and everything Jaya knows she learned from me. Her technology is worthless against me. And if it's that government agent? Well, let's say I have something special planned if he should show up."

"No, I have someone else to help me," said Dane, turning his head to either side. "Someone who should be helping me right... NOW!"

There was a moment where everyone, even the robots, were still and there was no noise other than the consoles and the robots.

"I said, right... NOW!"

Despite his dour mood, Honnenheim cracked a small smile. "I admit this part of your demise does amuse me."

Suddenly one of the nearby R-39 robots exploded in a flare of arcing superheated plasma. The robots all turned as another also exploded. All eyes turned to find Szandor standing on top of a stack of crates, holding a plasma cannon ripped from an R-39 he had bludgeoned into pieces.

"Sorry, I had to figure out how to fire this damn thing," said Szandor. "Funny thing, my aim sucks with real guns, but I'm awesome with this!"

Dane turned back to Honnenheim. "He's got you in his sights. So I suggest you surrender."

"Killing is not really your thing, Monday," said Honnenheim.

"I agree," said Dane. "But I'm not the one holding the plasma cannon. Over there is one pissed off young man who is not feeling the Christmas spirit either."

"And I grew up in Egan," called Szandor, focusing his gun on Honnenheim, the professor visibly realizing the implications of that statement.

"Well, I guess that I -" started Honnenheim, before spitting out, "ROBOTS FIRE!" and jumping out of his chair.

Plasma erupted from multiple guns as the room turned into a brilliant crossfire of superheated death. Szandor destroyed a few robots before their own shots disintegrated the pile of crates he jumped from. Rolling across the floor, he arose and started shooting. He felt as awesomely dangerous as he always thought of himself in his head, so for once reality matched his impressions. He also knew that he didn't have to feel guilty about destroying some robots, so he had plenty of pent-up frustration he could work out through the seriously overpowered plasma cannon.

Dane had also taken cover when everyone started firing, but he kept an eye on Honnenheim. Then he saw the professor shout, "Ready the sleigh!" When Honnenheim made a run for the sleigh, Dane was right behind him.

Honnenheim was just getting on the vehicle when Dane tackled him. They fell into the sleigh where they knocked against the R-39 who was in place for the swivel turret. The robot toppled over the side, leaving Dane and Honnenheim alone in the sleigh, engaging in an awkward grapple. Below them, the sleigh's propulsion systems kicked in, initially putting the sleigh into hover mode.

"Wait, where are you going?" said Szandor, working his way over to the central area, still under fire from robots. However, their ranks were thinning rapidly due to Szandor's own attacks.

"The console!" shouted Dane, as he struggled with Honnenheim. "Destroy the console!" Dane knew that the bombs across the city were being controlled from there.

"How?" said Szandor.

"Think of something!" said Dane with a gasp. He wasn't sure if Honnenheim had been working out or Dane was getting soft, but he was having trouble keeping the professor from going for the sleigh controls. It was slowly lifting from the ground into the sky.

Szandor looked around at the sizzling wrecks of many robots, but initially didn't see anything that could help him. Then he saw another red felt bag full of presents and knew there was only one way to do this. Well, one way that didn't leave him full of regret at missing the perfect opportunity. It was crazy, reckless, and would be cool in a movie, so of course it was just the thing Szandor Nowak would do.

Grabbing the sack full of present bombs, Szandor swung it around, using his hips and waist to great effect, finally letting go so that the bag of presents was thrown onto the console. Then he ran forward, jumping onto a crate and then from there leaping up to grab the last available piece of the lifting sleigh that was within reach and not expelling flames or fumes.

"What are you doing?" said Dane.

"I got this," said Szandor, turning to look down at the console. In his other hand he still held the plasma cannon. He aimed at the sack of presents on the console and pulled the trigger.

Plasma arced from the gun and hit the pile of presents. Even without the proper detonation signal, they were still quite volatile, particularly when struck by a stream of superheated plasma. The bombs exploded in a massive impact that sent roaring flames all over the warehouse. The rising sleigh rocked haphazardly from the concussive force. Szandor let the plasma cannon drop as he used both hands to hold on, loudly questioning his decision as the smoke and force from the explosion washed over him. Even Honnenheim and Dane stopped their melee to look down at the raging fire that now covered the remains of the console and the warehouse.

"Huh, I guess they were incendiary bombs," said Dane.

"Of course, did you not hear me call my plan *the burning terror*?" said Honnenheim.

They both looked at the raging flames below them and the fact that the sleigh had not yet risen entirely out of the burning warehouse.

"Uh, I say we have a truce until we get the sleigh out of danger," said Dane.

"Agreed," said Honnenheim, sitting down at the controls of the sleigh. Dane peered over Honnenheim's shoulder as the professor guided the sleigh up through the exit of the warehouse and then set it moving forward.

"Those controls look complicated," said Dane.

"Nonsense, they are quite easy. There is even an autopilot!" said Honnenheim.

"You're kidding!" said Dane, some of the awe in his voice faked, taking a quick look behind him.

"Of course not!" said Honnenheim. He flipped a switch and pressed a button. "This is the route by which I will bomb Avalon!"

"Yeah about that..." said Dane.

"Keep dreaming, old man," said Szandor.

He and Dane grabbed Honnenheim and pulled him out of the driver's seat, despite the professor's protests and struggle. The sleigh was picking up speed but was not at full velocity, so it was easy for them to hold Honnenheim over the side and drop him safely onto the top of a not too tall building. As they sped away, they could see the professor was unhurt as he stood at the building's edge shaking a fist at them and pledging their demise.

Soot smeared Szandor's face and clothes, but he otherwise looked okay. He collapsed into a slouch in the backseat. "I'm dying for a smoke," he said as he pulled out his pack of cigarettes.

Dane shook his head. "Don't smoke. It's a filthy habit that's going to kill you some day."

Szandor threw up his arms. "Even at dawn on Christmas in a rocket sleigh who knows how high above the city after destroying a whole battalion there's *still* someone giving me crap about smoking." But despite his words he put the cigarettes away. "So how *do* we get down from here? Jump?"

Dane shook his head again. "We're on autopilot right now. When we need to, I should be able to take us down safely. But this is the route Honnenheim was going to take, making a big circle around the city. I thought it might be nice to take a ride on autopilot for a while. It's not often you get to see a view like this." Dane looked out over Old Avalon, noting that the snow globe wasn't that far off from the real skyline.

Szandor nodded and stood up. He leaned over the edge of the sleigh, looking out on the city. He admitted it was a good view and probably not one he'd see otherwise. Even with the snow coming down, far more slowly than earlier, the city was beautiful. The view was only marred by smoke from the burning warehouse and the line of fire trucks making their way toward Asher. He could also see the decorations from everyone all over the city. There weren't quite as many lights on, as he realized that everyone was asleep, most ready to wake up on Christmas morning with a song in their heart, whether there was something under the tree for them or not.

Szandor watched longer, noticing how many holiday decorations were over the town. He realized how much effort people had put into celebrating, both in the more affluent areas and the poorer parts of Avalon. Soon dawn was breaking over the Husks to the east.

"I haven't always hated Christmas," said Szandor, still staring off the side at the city, Dane behind him looking off the other side of the sleigh. "I used to live for it when I was a kid."

"Something happened," said Dane. Not a question, a statement.

"Yeah," said Szandor. "I was ten years old. We never had a lot, but Mom really tried to make things the best they could be. She always tried the hardest at Christmas. She always tried to make sure we had decorations, at least a dinky tree, and something to open under that tree. But some years were better than others. And those other years were much worse.

"And I was selfish when I was ten. I know Christmas is supposed to be about giving and family, but I really wanted this one thing. I'm not sure why. Aggressive commercial marketing or something. I dropped a lot of hints, but I was ten. I had no idea how much it cost or if it was too much. But I really wanted it. It was the only thing I thought of when I saw Christmas coming."

"What was it?" asked Dane.

"You're going to laugh," said Szandor.

"Why would I laugh?" said Dane. "I won't laugh."

"It was an action figure," said Szandor. "The Red UltraRider. The one where he rides the Mechadragon. UltraRider had this laser sword and an arm that swung. The dragon shot these yellow plastic bits that were supposed to be lightning but were probably just recycled GI Joe missiles. It seemed awesome to a ten year old though." He paused. "Maybe I was too old for it. Maybe I should have asked for a cheap bike."

"And you didn't get it," said Dane.

"Of course I didn't get it," said Szandor. "I realize now that thing was too expensive for me to have asked for. It wasn't one of those $7 figures, it was the full on Mechadragon, it was like $100 or something. But I didn't know that. All I know is that I asked for it all year and didn't get it."

"What did you get?"

"Headphones and a cheap mp3 player... used, I think," said Szandor. "And a great gift, don't get me wrong, I used the crap out of that thing until it finally broke, and even then I got it fixed. I was inseparable from it for years. I really learned how great a gift it was. But... it wasn't the thing I wanted. I was so obsessed with one thing that when Christmas morning came and I didn't get it... well, I didn't handle myself well. I was a little jerk about it. To Mom, to Mikkel... to everyone. And while I know intellectually I was the jerk, all I remember is my family not understanding, being disappointed, that Christmas was a big waste. That's the Christmas where I learned I could shut everyone out with a pair of headphones.

"But regardless of the facts of the matter, the emotions stayed. I never liked Christmas after that," said Szandor. "I mean, I soon got to that age where I didn't like anything and I fought with anyone, but I never enjoyed Christmas after that year."

There was a long pause as they both looked out over the city. The warehouse fire was completely extinguished, but there was still some petulant smoke from the site.

"So why tell me this?" said Dane.

"I dunno," said Szandor. "This feels like the part on television where people suddenly get the Christmas spirit. That weird awkward part where everyone gets teary eyed and touchy feely. Like you're going to suddenly tell me there's a red UltraRider Mechadragon figure in that sack."

Dane took a quick look in the sack, tearing a few presents open. "No, just bombs."

Szandor gave a quick laugh. "It was stupid. A stupid hope. It's just Christmas. Nothing special happens on Christmas. I don't know why I had a glimmer of hope this year."

"What are you talking about?" said Dane. "Someone tried to bomb the city and set it on fire! A mad professor was trying to attack Christmas with robots and this rocket sleigh of death! And you disintegrated like a dozen robots with a plasma cannon! Now you're flying over the city in a probably illegal vehicle armed with advanced weaponry! That's really special!"

In spite of himself, Szandor smiled. "Y'know, you're right."

"And I know that you have a brother who loves you," said Dane. "I met the guy, I know he looks out for you. So you also have family waiting for you to spend the holidays with them. You got action, adventure, and family all in a twenty-four hour period. If that's not a great holiday, I don't know what is!"

Szandor looked out at the sun rising above the city. "You know, you're right. What am I being so sad and angsty about? Maybe I didn't get an UltraRider toy over a decade ago, but I spent the day with people who love me! And maybe my year and my life *has* been crappy, but it's my year and I've lived in the best I could! I've done some amazing things!"

"By George, I think he's found the Christmas spirit!" said Dane.

"Funny," said Szandor.

"And if you honestly don't want to spend so much time with family for whatever reason, you can come with me for Christmas," said Dane. "A bunch of us are getting together for a big feast."

"Nah, I appreciate the offer, but I don't want to hangout with a bunch of old guys."

"But -" started Dane.

"I think I'm ready to land," said Szandor. "I'm starving for some breakfast."

"Okay," said Dane. "But here's a random question - what do you think of Christmas hams?"

6

It wasn't easy finding a place open for breakfast on Christmas morning, but Szandor eventually found a deli that was willing to overcharge him for coffee and a bacon and egg sandwich. Szandor was in such a good mood that he didn't even make some snide comment when he paid.

Dane had indeed landed the sleigh, but he hadn't done it anywhere near where they wanted to land. So Szandor was on the north side of town making his way south. The subways were not in service and the roads were clogged even with low traffic, likely due to the Asher fire. The morning sun had begun to melt some of the snow that accumulated, giving the city an almost angelic look as the sunlight glittered off the buildings and the streets.

Szandor had eaten his sandwich on a bus bench, knowing that the buses weren't in service. Then he slurped on the coffee for a while, lost in thought and trying to gain a little courage. Then he took out his phone and dialed.

"Wha?" came the sleepy voice of his brother Mikkel.

"I wasn't sure if you were going to still be up or not," said Szandor.

"When Carly's here I get to sleep a little earlier," said Mikkel with a yawn. "In fact I would probably have gotten up in a little while. Well, maybe not on Christmas." He yawned again. "So what's up? Are you in trouble?"

"No," said Szandor. "Well, not anymore, at least. That's really not the point though. I wanted to call to... well... I'm going to come over for Christmas dinner today. If there's still a spot for me."

"Of course there's a spot for you," said Mikkel. "First off, we always have folding chairs. Second, you think you being crabby is really going to make me disinvite you to Christmas? You're my brother."

"Well, I also want to stop being so crabby," said Szandor. "Maybe this is a year to turn over a new leaf. Or something."

"Now I think I'm still asleep and dreaming all this," said Mikkel. "Hey Carly, Szandor's going to be a nice guy now. It's a Christmas miracle!"

"I... never mind," said Szandor. "I'll be over later, okay? I need to catch at least an hour or two of sleep first once I get home. Oh, and you may or may not be getting a delivery of a ham. He wasn't sure if they deliver today. I just wanted to warn you in case there's a mysterious ham."

"What?" said Mikkel. "Sure, I guess we could use some ham. Oh, and brother, bring some canned cranberries. We still need that."

"Oh yeah, I forgot about that," said Szandor. "Well, I'm across town. Someplace around here has gotta still be open."

Along his long walk home, Szandor managed to find a tiny Midtown minimart that was still open. According to their hours, they were due to close at two, but all Szandor cared was that they were open now. He grabbed a can of cranberries, then spent a minute or two looking at their beer selection before deciding it was too early to drink. Or late, since he had been up all night.

He joined the line for the cash register. Being one of the few places open meant there was a long line of people who had forgotten things for their holiday feast. The man in front of him had only a roll of tinfoil. Szandor stood in line for a while, humming and wishing he had some headphones.

"Szandor?" The voice was familiar, but he hadn't heard it in a long time. Still, even after this long absence it still gave him a pleasant flutter in his chest.

He turned and saw behind him in line his former coworker Yasmin. They had worked together at a call center until Szandor had been fired when he had to lay low. There had always been a spark of attraction between them, but circumstances never worked out. They were supposed to talk, but he had never been able to get in touch with her due to the firing. He had thought about her a few times, but when he finally had enough courage to go to the office, he learned from Rhys that Yasmin had taken a job elsewhere.

As he looked at her, he saw that she was as pretty as he had remembered, even if she was wrapped up for the cold weather. He had missed that smile far more than he admitted.

"What happened to you?" said Yasmin, her smile lapsing into concern. "Is that ash on your face?"

Szandor absentminded rubbed his cheek. He smiled. "It's been a crazy night. Hell, a crazy year."

"I know that feeling," said Yasmin. Then she looked down at his hands and cocked her head. A strange smile crossed her face. Then she raised her hand, showing the only item she was buying. A can of cranberries. "I guess you forgot the cranberries too."

Maybe it was the early hour, maybe it was the long night, maybe it was seeing Yasmin again, or maybe it was just a touch of the Christmas spirit, but Szandor smiled and they laughed.

Perhaps this would be a much better Christmas after all.

About the Author

Dennis Liggio is the author of sixteen books, including I
KILL MONSTERS, the DAMNED LIES series, THE LOST AND
THE DAMNED, and the books set in the city of New Avalon. He is a
veteran of the game industry, enjoys long walks on the beach while
thumbing through tomes of unspeakable evil, and rumor has it that if
you say his name three times in front of a mirror at midnight he will
appear and give you Hostess Fruit Pies. He writes primarily in the
genres of geeky absurdist humor, horror, and urban fantasy. He lives in
Pflugerville, Texas with his amazing wife, awesome daughter, and four
cats that act like wieners.

www.dennisliggio.com

Books by Dennis Liggio

I Kill Monsters (Nowak Brothers #1)

Mikkel and Szandor kill monsters.

So what if they're making it up as they're going along? How much
do you need to know to bash in a zombie's head with a lead pipe or
slice a ghoul with an internet-bought katana?

They may in fact have no clue what they're doing.

But if you need someone to go down into the sewers to clear out
some monsters, figure out why everyone in your neighborhood is
getting bitten, or if you swear you really saw a zombie and you don't

know who to call, then call them. They'll show up in their van of makeshift weapons, gear, and cleaning supplies to investigate your problem. They may be twenty-somethings with their own issues, but when it comes to monsters they know what they're doing.

They probably have no clue what they're doing.

That has never stopped them before.

Hired by a woman from the rich side of town who believes she's being stalked by monsters, the two brothers think they've finally gotten an easy job that will pay well. But as they follow the clues, nothing adds up. Kidnappings, jackbooted commandos, and mysterious emails are just the beginning. Soon they find themselves involved in something bigger than monsters. It's anybody's guess whether they'll come through it alive, much less get paid.

Manic Monday (Dane Monday #1)

Dane Monday deals with weird stuff. Mad scientists, sorcerers, robots, time-travelling cats, cyborgs learning the concept of love, and more. Whether it's a death ray, a doomsday ritual, or simply magic gone wrong, Dane Monday is there to stop them. He's even got a rogue's gallery of megalomaniacal villains who want revenge. Armed only with his wits, some reluctant allies, and a satchel full of gadgets, Dane steps forward to save the city of New Avalon.

While investigating an abandoned building, Dane encounters the remnants of a magical ritual shortly before the building explodes in spectacular fashion. Narrowly escaping this destruction with his new ally, the aspiring journalist Abby Connors, Dane follows the threads of this mystery while evading a menagerie of homicidal robots, kidnapping thugs, and the wrath of a mad scientist. At the bottom of it all is a scheme to destroy New Avalon involving a century-old architect, a historic hotel, and something not of our world.

Can Dane and Abby brave the dangers and the strangeness to save the city of New Avalon? Find out in Manic Monday!

Damned Lies

Damned Lies is the true story of things that never happened. It is a fictional memoir of fantastic events. It is a chronicle of self-cloning, of adventure, of magic, of bare-fisted hobo boxing tournaments, of zombies, and more. It's the autobiography of a wild summer adventure out beyond the fields we know. It's the secret of what's hidden in a government bunker, it's the story of helping a nun with a crossbow hunt a vampire, it's the explanation of why you can't have that death ray you really wanted. It's a cautionary tale of just why cloning yourself is a really terrible idea.

Damned Lies is a big fish story for those who don't fish. It's a shaggy dog story for cat lovers. It's the scifi fantasy humor memoir we'll all wish we dictated on our deathbed. It's why we can't have nice things.

Damned Lies is just the first book in the Damned Lies series, a chronicle of fantastic adventures. It is followed by two sequels: Damned Lies Strike Back, the memoirs of the narrator's college years and his war with his homicidal clone's Lovecraftian cult, and Damned Lies of the Dead 3D, the memoir of Austin, Texas's zombie outbreak of 1995.